Sorcery and Kings

Mary Catelli

Published by Wizard's Wood Press, 2019.

SORCERY AND KINGS

First edition. October 16, 2019.

Copyright © 2019 Mary Catelli.

ISBN: 978-1-942564-67-6

Written by Mary Catelli.

The Hall of the Heiress

She had no memory of how she had come to be there, let alone where she had been before.

She did not remember so much as walking into the house, or waking up there. She did not know how she had slowly grown aware of its features, though she vaguely recalled being mindful of some before she was mindful of others.

The sea-green house sat by the sea. Cupolas and towers dotted it, and all its windows were either round or tall, with arched tops. A bridge stretched out from the house itself to a summer house, intricately and geometrically adorned, larger in itself than many a house where whole families lived (and she knew that though she had no memory of ever seeing such houses or such families). Below the bridge, at low tide, a rocky valley, with sides of reddish cliffs, spread with a thin trickle of water; she could see, off in the distance, a waterfall at the end of the valley.

At high tide, the valley held waves and seawater, and winged sea serpents, as sea-green as the house, sported in it.

If, that was, the sea serpents were real.

The wall about the house was real. Towering and solid and without a single door, stretching out into the sea on either hand, into the waters that were deeper than she was tall. To walk about the wall, and along the seashore, was the work of less than an hour, and it held her confined here, in reality.

She had her doubts about the rest. Except the apple orchard beside the summer house, with trees laden with apples, and holding some birdhouses of intricate ornament. And the moon

rising from it every night. Sometimes it was full, with a rotund face, with closed eyes; sometimes it was an impossible crescent, arching far past the middle, and a sharp nose from the narrow face that looked outward; always the moon actually rose up between the branches, and when it was a crescent, birds perched on it.

She thought it was too strange to be unreal. Falsity would have tried harder to look real.

Even the arched main door into the house, with its inscription "The Hall of the Heiress," might be unreal. If it meant what it said, the heiress could be none other than herself. She did not know if she believed it, she certainly did not know whom she had inherited from, or what she had inherited, but she wandered freely over the house. Up stairs of malachite, and down stairs of marble. Into a bedchamber—the lone bed chamber of a house that could hold, in comfort, a family of twenty and all their servants—a bedchamber with floors of mother-of-pearl, a bed like a half-opened shell, and walls of silver and green in rounded geometry.

All the ornaments of the house were geometrical. No leaves or flowers, no beasts or birds—no fish, however fitting they would be, or even anything she could convince herself was meant to be a wave—though in the garden, where there was a great pond instead of flowers, two swans drifted over the waters.

When she woke in one morning filled with gray light, she stared at the pale green ceiling as minutes inched by. She sighed and pondered why she was kept here. Whether this house was, in itself, her inheritance. Whether it was a test of some kind before she was declared an heiress. Whether, perhaps, she was kept prisoner here so that someone else could inherit because she had failed some task or did not arrive at some ceremony.

She sighed again. She had learned nothing to tell which, if any, were true, but, however familiar the house, she did not know it so well that she could swear that she could not escape.

All the garments in the wardrobe fit perfectly, she noted, and tried to ponder that as she dressed. But she had already guessed that she was the heiress. She could deduce nothing new from the clothes before she laced up her gown. And nothing more when she descended the stairs to find the kitchen, in its blue tile, where a pot of oatmeal sat steaming with no sign of a servant or of a fire.

She supposed she could feel more alarmed at that, or the way she had found no larder, and so she was at the mercy of whatever cooked now (the house itself?), and might not cook in the days to come. Still, it seemed the sort of thing that befit a house with sea serpents swimming about. She sat at the kitchen table, and ate her oatmeal, which seemed implausibly ethereal to taste.

Having forced down the last bite, she pushed the bowl away to start her search.

She tried the library first, to read, to learn if it said what this house was, or how she had come there, or whether she could escape. She had not great hope when she walked in. An exquisite little library, with a bay window bedecked with gold, chairs here and there, and three bookcases done with scrollwork, not a stride long and no higher than her waist. No more. Every shelf held books from end to end, but they could not hold enormous knowledge in so limited a compass.

She told herself that she only needed one that covered the right subject. Even only one with the right page. A history book that told her of a secret passage, a book of natural philosophy that explained how to get the sea serpents to carry her away, a spell book that told her how to fly away—or restore her memory, and learn its secrets that way. She did not know that she had not known much of the house; she could have known all about it, and lost that memory with the rest.

She crouched by the first bookcase.

None of the tomes had titles on their spines. With a grimace, she started to pull the books out, looking to see if they might help.

Time and again, the words jumbled into meaninglessness before her gaze, or dissolved into melodious but vacuous words, or turned to mist in her thoughts as soon as she lifted her face from the page.

On the twentieth work, she put the book firmly away. She thought that none of them talked of her inheritance, but when she could not read the words, that did not matter. The only question now was how she might escape. If the books would not tell her, she had to find out for herself.

She looked out the bay window at the sea. How far it stretched, out to a cloudy horizon. Sea serpents sported in it, even at low tide. She did not want to risk it, if they were guardians to keep her captive. She let her breath out and turned her face way. At least—not first of all.

Swans, she thought. She hurried across the room and looked into the garden. They too might be dangerous, but she had to undertake some risk.

* * *

The birds ignored her as she stripped off her clothes by the pool side.

She thought of dipping her toe into the waters, but it would not matter how cold they were, and she could see how deep they went. She drew a deep breath and dived in, swimming down, down, down. To a pool bottom that was as solid as the wall.

Again and again she dived, until she had searched every inch of it and found no outlet hidden under the ripples.

Finally she dragged herself up on the bank and sat, shivering, to dry before she dressed herself again. The swans ignored her—though she noted, now, that their idle gliding across the waters had always avoided where she might surface.

Her gaze went to the wall. She had checked that. . . .

She blinked. She did not quite remember checking it. Any more than she remembered realizing it was there.

Her hair was still sodden. She stood and dressed, and let the hair fall down her back like damp seaweed, before she walked about the house and crossed the bridge. The tide was so high that the waves engulfed the entire valley, and licked at the stone of the bridge.

She forced herself to look ahead to the summer house. And then to walk by it, to the wall, and search it for secret doors and trick entrances.

That side of the valley was easy enough, especially since she did not risk the pounding waves by venturing into the sea. Every inch was solid, and nothing protruded or sank back in a way that might conceal a secret.

Crossing back over the bridge gave her enough wall that when she had worked her way around, back to the sea, the tide was low again. Sea water lapped on the rocky shore. She eyed it, slipped off her shoes and stockings, and hiked up her skirts. If she went too deep, she would have to shed her clothes as she had for the pool, or drown when the seawater dampened them, and they started to pull her down. . . but for now she edged into the sea.

A thundering roar echoed from wall and stone. A sea serpent, its wake frothing from its speed, charged toward her. She squeaked and fled, not even stopping for her shoes. Water and foam, pushed up before the serpent, engulfed her feet again and again, and once or twice she stumbled in it, but she clambered up to the front steps. As she reached the front door, she pulled it open, and turned enough to see the sea serpent withdrawing out to sea, and all the sea water with it.

She grimaced. No pale dots lay on the shore to mark her stockings, nor dark ones to mark her shoes. The sea serpent had borne them, at least, out to sea.

Her bedchamber had more stockings and more shoes. She walked up to it, and the wardrobe. She washed salt and sand from her feet, dried them again, and put on stockings and shoes. The new time to ponder why it all fit revealed nothing to her. Neither as to why they fit, nor as to what she could do next.

The hallway outside bore no tracks of damp sand. She turned away and descended the back stair, all dark green with black railings. When she reached the ground, she hesitated. Steps went further downward. She remembered there being basements below, but she did not remember searching them.

She certainly did not remember looking for a secret passageway out.

She looked about. And tried to remember. Was there a candlestick, or a candle in it, in all this house? Or any other lamp that she could carry below? A lantern would be best, but she remembered nothing in all the house.

She bit her lip. The corridor she was in was lit by windows, with pearly gray light. So had every other room she had walked in. She did not think she had seen a single lamp in all the hall.

But, if she had learned of the basement, there had to be some light down there. Or a way to fumble back up from the gloom. Her tongue touched her lip. Then, if she found no light below, she knew that her memories of it were false. Her mouth twisted a little. Their falsity would not surprise her, though not a memory had proven false yet.

The door opened easily and soundlessly. A light glowed, down below. She took the railing—black wrought iron—and started down, as slow and stately as if she were entering a royal ball on the arm of a king.

The basement looked simple enough. Stout stone, the blocks very large, mortared together. No great barrels of ale. No stacks of corded firewood.

She was looking not for a larder, she reminded herself, but for an escape. She went to the wall.

Testing the stone was the only way to search. There was no stone lighter, or darker, than the rest. Nothing blocked up with bricks. Nothing even arched as if a doorway had gone beneath. Her mouth tightened. Inch by inch, she edged around the basement, and found every inch solid enough to keep her captive.

She walked back to the stairs. Only at them did she turn and look back. The stone was solid, unbroken. She could not see where the light came from, though she looked everywhere twice.

Her hand tightened on her skirts. If she had even a hint, she would have hunted it down and seen if she could get out where light could get in. But she had not.

And—if light could get in here so—who knew? There might be a secret passageway out in the middle of the house. Who knew? Perhaps in a wall clearly as thin as paper, there was a passage.

Her fingers brushed against the wall.

Lunch first, she told herself. And a good solid one.

In the kitchen, she ate delicate fish of a kind she had never seen before, and a garnet-red fruit she had never seen before, and slices of bread from a grain strange to her, and was glad she could wash it down with water. Still, it filled the stomach by the time she cleared her plate.

She pushed the chair back and began in the kitchen, searching the fireplace and the wall by it. (She tried to not flinch when the plate vanished as soon as she turned her back.)

Her fingers traced out every trace of the kitchen tile without finding any unevenness, and when she pushed, nothing moved. She sighed. Along the corridor, into the sitting rooms—she paused to peer into a grandfather clock, one that clearly was free-standing before returning to the walls—and other rooms whose purpose was not so clear.

She wished for pen and paper, to map, but the floor was not a labyrinth, and before the afternoon was half over, she had gone through every room, checking every wall.

Sea serpents jumped from the water in great leaps below the bridge, the tide not being high enough for them to swim under. She sighed. There was only the upper floors, then. And she should not feel that relieved to know that once that was done, and proved fruitless, she had carried out her search.

One sea serpent leapt up, flew over the bridge, and landed on the other side. She closed her eyes. For a moment, she wished that she could hop on the back of one and make it fly off. Or at least bear her over the waves, across the seven seas, to—elsewhere. She walked off, toward the stairs, and told herself that it might not be large enough to carry her.

Library, which made her shift the bookcases about, and pull out all the books in hope that the back of the bookcase was a way. Bedchamber, where she spent more time on the wardrobe than the walls, and checked under the bed. Other rooms, unfurnished, of uncertain purpose. All, all, all devoid of any semblance of a secret way out.

One back corridor had stairs that led up to the attic. She looked at it. Towers first, she decided. The small rooms had more walls.

She climbed to the first, a room decidedly round, and eyed the small, round windows. From them, she could see the walls were too thin for her to walk in any passage between them.

She searched, none the less. And, finding nothing, went on to the next tower.

But her searches there found only rooms round or octagonal or square, with ceilings that conformed to the roof, and so no space of another. And every one of them had sound walls.

She circled back to the attic.

A door there seemed to lead to a corridor that had no place to fit in the house. Her heart hammered with uncommon force as if, for all her searching, she had not even imagined it could be true, that there could be an escape. She fumbled along the green stone way, until it led out again, back in the attic.

Despair washed over her. Her shoulders slumped. She lacked even the energy to throw herself to floor, or to wail her heart out.

Slowly, slowly, she trudged the rest of the way about the attic, finding nothing. Not even chests filled with old things to divert herself with, let alone a door.

The grandfather clock rang the hour of seven as she descended the stairs.

Dinner, she told herself. Bed after. She eased her way back toward the kitchen.

A round window looked out on the pool. She sighed. A garden would have given her something to while the time away. Flowers would be best, but topiary would have been some diversion. Not just this sight of endlessly swimming swans. They floated within a stride of the edge, and looked toward the rising moon. . . .

The door stood beside her. She yanked it open, ran out on the flagstones, thought that not shedding her clothes raised the danger of drowning (but only for a moment, she had no time), threw herself into the pool where the swans were.

They started, but not swiftly enough. She had her arms across their necks.

They cried out, they flapped their wings, they took to the air—and she did not let go. They bore her up into the air, forward, where they faced—toward the moon. She kept her gaze intent on it.

Their flight barely reached it, but she leapt. The wings flapped behind her, but she did not turn from the metallic moon, and landed on it. Her arms went out to clutch it close.

The bottom curve arched enough to hold her. Her arms would grow stiff, but the swans flitted away, and the moon slowly rose higher. She swallowed. She had escaped, one way or another.

After a moment, the moon opened its eyes. Its voice was dry, ironic. "This is an odd one. Do you not appreciate the Hall of the Heiress?"

"This is how I always show how much I appreciate a hall," she said.

The moon chuckled. After another moment, she eyed it. "What is it?"

The moon lifted an eyebrow.

"The hall. Is it to keep an heiress from claiming her inheritance properly? Is it a test to see if the heiress is fit?"

The moon's mouth arched into a half-smile.

"Is it the inheritance? No wonder I was sent there without my knowledge if so. I would have declined the honor."

"Such mistrust, o heiress. It is meant to keep you safe. So many perils beset an heiress."

Moments inched by.

"Safe," she said bitterly.

"Did you, in all your searches, find a skeleton of another heiress?"

She shifted her weight around so she could look down. The house was shrinking below, but she could still see the sea serpents, frolicking as if they did not care about her escape. Perhaps they did not. Her mouth twisted. Perhaps they were not her guardians after all.

"No."

The moon shifted a little, as if it shrugged.

"To refuse the safety is to refuse the inheritance," it said, idly. "So I can not call you heiress. Have you another name?"

"Serena," she said, and blinked. It was her name. She wondered whether, if she had pondered the question while in the house, she would have remembered it. She wondered how much more could be remembered if she were asked the right question. Perhaps merely seeing things would jog loose the memories stolen from her.

"Serena, then," said the moon. "I set on the other side. It's not in a house. It's in a wide-open field, with forest and villages about."

"And roads?" said Serena.

"Yes," said the moon.

She nodded. And then leaned back against the moon, to wait for a road to take.

The Firemaster and the Flames

Ahead in the forest, flickering orange light turned pines to silhouettes, and voices sounded among the trunks. Jan bit her lip, even though she heard no panic. No easy path around that—

"Fiah!" Elena wriggled, leaning forward in Jan's arms. Jan sighed, shifted Elena's weight, and walked on. The air smelled of pine and smoke, and the way brightened until she could see the flames, licking the air, and as tall as she was. Sparks flew, orange in the gray smoke.

At the base of the fire, a fireling no bigger than Elena's hand stood, like a smaller flame, like a vague human with its legs joined where it touched the wood. It threw fiery, fingerless hands into the air. Plumes of smoke and flame soared, but firemasters in their yellow smocks had already encircled the blaze. Their faces were gilded with its light.

Jan breathed a sigh of relief; they did not need her when she had her hands full. She still had to wait to get through. She shifted Elena.

The firemasters' hands moved, and the flames turned back to the burned-out earth. The fireling squealed in tremulous rage, and sparks flooded outward from all the flame.

Jan put her free hand up to cast a small spell. Sparks doubled back. Elena thrashed, trying to snatch them from the air. And the firemasters' spells closed in on the fireling. Tiny black dots like eyes opened wide, for a moment.

Hands rose into the air and plunged downward, like a knife cutting.

The fire blinked out. Darkness and cool air rushed in, and Clarice's voice came sharply from the gloom. "What brought you here, Jan?"

"Going home," said Jan, tartly. Elena squeaked.

Someone chuckled. A glow sprung up from one firemaster's hand, gilding their faces again.

"Good thing we caught you." Clarice put her hands on her hips. "You're wanted at the station. Someone's coming on the train—" She smiled, unpleasantly. "Might be here now."

Jan's eyes narrowed. Clarice might claim, afterward, that Jan had mistaken her, despite all the witnesses.

"Hurry, lass," said the white-haired Nan. "They sounded—urgent."

Jan's gaze went past her. Through the branches, she saw the station lights, atop the bowl that formed Firerock. She faced a steep hike. Sworn duty, she reminded herself.

Elena burbled, and Jan fought down a sigh. She didn't have time reach home first, and she couldn't leave Elena anyway. She strode past Clarice's smirk, to the green stairs doubling back and forth on the slope.

At the top, Jan stepped out of the way and stood to regain her breath. Elena looked about with wide eyes and in merciful silence. The station held no trains, but the last one must have discharged passengers, not long ago. Brown-haired or blond, the travelers glanced at the red-haired souls who worked at the station—or the one with another one, a child, in her arms.

No one seemed to look for her.

A train whistle resounded through the trees, and a train thundered in. Elena wailed, and Jan bounced her on her shoulder.

A grizzled ticket seller looked at her as passengers swarmed from the train. His mouth quirked, and wordless, he pointed at the waiting room. Esmond—Esmond himself—stalked out, looking ready to lecture, once again, on how the firemasters served the king and obeyed his officials.

He glared at Elena. "Did no one tell you that this is important?"

"I had gotten Elena from my aunt. Do you want me to lug her back there and return?"

Esmond snorted. "When Lord Bertram has just disembarked?"

Jan glanced back. In the crowd, one passenger stood out. He had dressed soberly for travel, but the cloth was finer than most people wore for festivals. A young man, also well-dressed, came behind him.

"Just well," said Jan, coldly. "Aunt Cecily goes to bed once I take Elena."

Her gaze went past Lord Bertram, to the baggage car, where she saw something else. "I wish—"

She handed Elena to Esmond—making him gape, and Elena look wide-eyed—and stalked to the baggage car. There, she pulled out a ragged bundle. The baby inside began to cry. Little scraps of hair showed red-gold through the gaps in the cloth.

Jan touched the cheek and felt how chilled the baby was. She juggled him into the crook of her arm so she could raise one hand and cast a spell. Air glowed like candlelight and grew warmer, but the baby wailed on, more earnestly. She walked back slowly, and had to slow still further twice, to keep the glow and warmth following.

"I suppose that it can not be a fire demon," said Lord Bertram, softly, if not so softly as he seemed to think.

"If it were, sir," said the young man with him, equally softly, "best to leave it in a firemaster's hand."

Jan closed the distance.

"So!" said Esmond. "You found yourself another foundling!"

"Elena takes up enough of my time—or so you complain." Jan reached out to take Elena and dump the baby in Esmond's hands. "Since I am needed, you must take him to the orphanage. He can be fostered in the morning." The baby screamed.

"This is a matter of royal service," said Lord Bertram. He eyed her, the belted yellow smock, and the breeches underneath.

Firemasters, thought Jan, have to run. Wizards wear robes because they can afford to look solemn and stately, not needing to make haste.

"We must raise our successors," said Jan, coldly. "The king will need them."

After a moment, Lord Bertram scowled. "You smell of smoke! What have you left? If there is danger—"

"That fire is done with. I had just arrived here myself, because no one would cease their magics to tell me of your arrival, until it was gone." She hefted Elena. "I have to put Elena to bed, or she'll wail while you talk."

Lord Bertram's scowl deepened. "Surely, some woman can look after the child."

"You mistake me for a fine noblewoman, with servants," said Jan. Or a wizard, she thought.

"Go," said Esmond, coldly. "We will come to your house."

"Bring my books when you come," said Jan. "They would have come on the train, and it would delay me to fetch them."

* * *

Down in the valley, two red-gold heads, a woman and a child disappeared, into the darkness of the trees. Esmond snorted.

"I assure you, Lord Bertram, Master Colin, that I do not inflict this woman on you out of spite. She is a *master* of fire and knows wizardry as well. At least, some wizardry. But—" He shook his head. "I wrestled with my choice. Imagine, she feigns that that child is a foundling! She claims some wizard conjured it to her hearth!"

Colin raised an eyebrow. Conjuring a baby to a hearth would take skill and knowledge, but it could be done.

Esmond turned aside. "You!" A young, strawberry-blond woman blinked at him. He dumped the baby in her arms. "The orphanage."

She scurried off.

"At least that one is safe," said Lord Bertram, gravely. "Through the king's providence in having the red-haired young brought here—through his parents' obedience."

Esmond's mouth twitched.

"Your Mistress Jan seems to overlook that the baby was fortunate not to have been taken for a fire demon."

"She knows that," said Esmond. He shouted for a porter. "The books for Mistress Jan!" An auburn-haired man scurried over with three books.

"I am sure, Master Colin, that you can carry them," said Esmond.

Colin eyed the titles. Books of wizardry: a simple text on wards, and two tomes unfamiliar to him. He slung the books under his arm. Fortunate that they did not need this Mistress Jan for her skill with wizardry.

As they climbed down the stairs, Esmond said, "She spends a foolish amount of money on those books. She was always fond of babies—but she was always fond of books, too. Put off the young men. If not *entirely*."

"If," said Lord Bertram, "she can deal with fires, we can deal with her—quirks." He glanced at Esmond's dark brown hair. "I am sure you are His Royal Majesty's faithful servant, but you are no firemaster."

Esmond plodded down the last stairs in silence. Then he said, "No. I am no firemaster."

Esmond cast a spell, and light glowed in a little circle about them. Tree trunks loomed, casting enormous shadows on the trees behind, and holding their boughs too high to be quite seen. As they walked along the path, branches blocked the lights from the station, and forest engulfed them. Even their footfalls made little sound on the soft earth. The light vanished swiftly, and shadows danced about them as they passed tree after tree.

Colin forced his breath out. "Must not have been a fire here lately." The forest swallowed up the sound. "Look at the trees. I've seen churches with smaller pillars."

"Pines," said Esmond. "They grow quickly."

Still, thought Colin, these were not the growth of a year or two.

Birches appeared ahead, with snow-white bark, and stout trunks. Next to them, a house stood built of stone. Light glowed from its windows, and its door stood ajar. "That's Jan's."

"Old," said Lord Bertram.

"Quite. An old family of firemasters." Esmond snorted. "In no danger of extinction."

Inside, a vast fireplace stood in one wall, empty of fire and ash alike. An open door to a side room showed Jan leaning over a cradle. The air about her glowed, which shone into the room, over the table—long for a lone woman and one child—and the books along the wall.

"Put the books on the table," Jan called, without looking up. "And close the door."

Colin laid the books aside and eased over to the bookcases, looking quickly. An—eclectic collection of wizardry. Some books were more commonly the province of master wizards than students, but he wondered if she even knew any ward spells.

The light shifted, and he turned to see Jan coming out, her narrowed eyes intent on him, and the bookcase. Without a word, she turned to the table.

* * *

"Master Esmond recommended you," said Lord Bertram. "You have fought firelings—and even fire demons, I have heard."

"True enough." Jan sat back, watching him warily. Royal officials seldom meant good news. She wished she was not so tired and could increase the light spell, or had had time to start a fire before they arrived. Darkness filled the windows, seeming to press on her spell, to encroach on her.

"One may have escaped Firerock."

For a moment, Jan did not twitch. Throwing out such an accusation—she let her breath out and spoke, her voice cool and serene.

"I doubt that. An escaped fireling would leave a trail of smoke and ash that anyone could trace. You would not need a firemaster. Not even to notice its escape from Firerock." She met Lord Bertram's gaze and wondered how she had managed the voice.

Colin sat back; she could not read his face.

"Then," said Lord Bertram, "one has been summoned. Or there is another fire spot. Each of which seems less likely."

After a moment pondering, Jan sighed. "If there is a fireling, one *is* true."

"We hope it's no larger than a fireling," said Colin.

"Has no one *seen* it?" said Jan. When Colin shook his head, her mouth twisted. Such confidence. She wondered what they wanted a firemaster for, when they knew so much.

Lord Bertram said, quickly, "There have been many blazes, all with no source. If it is not a fireling, we are baffled." He spread his hand. "Master Esmond said you knew wizardry."

"Some." She could feel the presence of her handful of books, behind her—and knew how few any wizard would regard them, and how much they held that she had yet to study.

"The fireling," said Colin, "has struck, more than once, near the university at Bridgewood."

Jan blinked. Susannah, she thought. For a moment, her face twisted; she flattened it out and wondered what it had shown or, for that matter, what she had felt. A welter of emotions, she knew. She forced her breath out. They did not know that she had reason to feel, after such news. She had taken care about that. Two of them did not even know her sister had left Firerock to marry, and live at Bridgewood.

"His Majesty thinks," said Lord Bertram, "that the wizards are not, after all, firemasters."

"Wise of him," said Jan. She could see which way this went. She supposed it could have been worse. "It is an *honor* to serve the king," she added dryly.

"I have come," said Lord Bertram, "to impress on you the gravity of what you must do: end the fires."

"A long journey, then," said Jan. It was not as if she had a choice, but she did not have to go as meek as a lamb. "I shall bring Elena. I dare say the university can provide quarters for a young child, too."

Lord Bertram's eyes narrowed. "This is a matter of some importance, Mistress Jan."

"So is raising young firemasters," said Jan. "A royal duty, in fact. My aunt is too old and frail to look after Elena day and night."

"This will not do," said Lord Bertram.

"Many firemasters can deal with even a fire demon," said Jan, "and the university can hardly need *my* spells, with their wizards."

Lord Bertram sighed. "I dare say they can find you a nursemaid, even if you leave on the dawn train."

Jan blinked. He did intend to ensure she went, then. She had thought he would not yield so easily, if at all.

"You are, after all, in His Majesty's employ."

Slowly, she said, "I must prepare, or I will not be ready."

Lord Bertram rose. "Young Colin here was once a student at the university. Not a master wizard, but a wizard."

Colin looked back at her, his dark eyes unreadable.

"He shall send word of your needs and conduct you, and cast any spells needed to smooth the way. I am sure that the matter rests in good hands, and you have no need of a royal official to peer over your shoulder."

Jan smiled and knew it did not reach her eyes. It was not for her comfort that he left her. "You will have arranged for where he will spend the night, Master Esmond."

* * *

The morning was gray—charcoal gray, but not black—and Colin looked into the valley, filled with mists like a bowl with porridge.

"You will fly down to see her, then?" said Master Esmond.

Colin thought he meant to sound jocular. He smiled, thinly. "I could hardly see the house through the leaves."

Esmond blinked, as if wondering whether he jested.

Colin strode down the stairs. Perhaps he could make out Jan's house from the air—with all the pines surrounding that grove of birches—but flying was not so easy as walking.

The forest was far more pleasant by day. Birds sang, and the air smelled sweetly. Under gaps in the branches, dew lay thickly on the earth. Low houses of stone, so mossy that he did not feel surprised he had missed them last night, stood among the trees, as if watching against fires.

Gray morning light spilled over Jan's house and the birches. Elena cooed next to three bags. Her back to the path, Jan raised her hands. Colin watched her gestures, heard her words, and stood like a statue.

When she turned away, he found his voice. "The Hieronymus Ward, wasn't it?"

Jan nodded.

"How did you *learn it*?"

"From a book." Jan picked up Elena. "It seemed suitable for my purposes."

"Gray-bearded masters find it difficult," said Colin. Elena wriggled in Jan's arms to peer at him. He went to pick up two bags—tentatively, but they came up with ease. Jan had either packed lightly or used wizardry.

"Don't wait until your hair is gray," said Jan. "Try it with a child underfoot. That inspires."

He raised an eyebrow. And yet she wanted a simple book on wards.

* * *

In the gray morning light, as the mists melted, the train rattled through fields and orchards. Colin sat by the window and watched them go by. Finally, he said, "All the farmers are red-haired."

"They can't farm inside Firerock," said Jan. "Too many fires. Too much risk, even." Elena scampered about the benches.

"Don't you teach them to be firemasters?" said Colin.

"We try," said Jan. "When we fail—did you think the ticket sellers were firemasters?"

Colin's mouth twitched.

"And who did you think sold us our food?"

He said, dryly, "I have heard wizards are not overly welcome at Firerock. I doubt anyone I know could have told me."

Jan's mouth worked for a moment before easing. "True enough. Did you see why, while you were at Firerock?"

Colin eyed her. Another thing he would never had learned, that.

"Firerock is a perfect bowl in shape." Jan leaned forward. "A wizard once thought she could contain the fire spot."

Colin glanced back—as if he could see now—but he remembered how the walls had dipped down, and then flattened.

"What spell did she use?"

"Good heavens," said Jan, sitting back, "tell mere firemasters *that*? And after, it was impossible to ask. It was the firemasters—and others—that we pitied."

She watched his mouth, but then, he had nothing to say to that.

"We'll have to see what your wizards can do with firemastery."

* * *

On a bench, Elena slept so soundly that she did not stir when the train trundled into a station. Peasants clumped on the platform; the women wore brightly embroidered shawls on their heads, and the men, felt caps in vivid colors. They pressed into the train, and a young woman walked toward where Colin and Jan sat, calling, "There's room down here!"

At the doorway, she stopped, her hand still on the latch. Her eyes grew enormous before she ran back.

Jan sighed. "Did you see her hair?"

Colin shook his head.

"Blond. But at some places, that touch of red would have sent her to Firerock."

* * *

All the train cars were full, even crowded, except theirs.

The train crossed a river. Water lilies blossomed white in the backwaters, two swans floated serenely down it, and Elena leaned against the window, staring and leaving smudges. Jan sat quietly beside her, looking at the river for the brief glimpse where it was clear. Moments later the willows on its shores had hidden the water from view.

She seemed calmer than when she was first wrested away from Firerock, and Elena seemed fascinated enough with the window to ignore them both.

"I know that you—that few firemasters ever leave Firerock, and never for long," said Colin.

Jan did not twitch. The words did not come any more easily.

"I don't—you can't have known—wizards can't help—"

Jan did not blink.

Colin could not meet her gaze. "Wizards send their red-haired children to Firerock, like everyone else."

"Let me show you something." Jan rummaged through her bag and pulled out a candle.

"Ooo." Elena skittered across the car. Jan grabbed her with her free hand and handed Colin the candle. "Now, do this." She showed him some gestures and had him recite a spell.

"Now put them together."

Colin shrugged and obeyed. The wick flared with a tiny blue flame; it grew and turned yellow, except where it touched the wick and still burned blue—a perfectly ordinary candle flame. He could feel the heat spreading from it. He stared for a minute; then, with his free hand, he pulled a lock of his hair forward. It was still dark.

"Some children don't stay redheads," said Jan, "their hair turns blond or brown—especially the babies—but they can master fire. My father had hair as dark as yours. You must have seen that we were only *mostly* red-haired, at Firerock."

"Actually," said Colin, "I saw every shade from auburn to strawberry blond—but all red." He blew out the flame. Smoke curled grayly up from the wick, its scent stronger on the air than when it had burned. "A few dozen—I will take your word for it that there are more."

He handed back the candle. "If you turn wizards into firemasters, *what* will be the fate of red-haired children? They will not be *needed* as firemasters at Firerock."

Jan smiled sadly and slipped the candle away. "Why, we will become farmers. Or wizards, perhaps."

* * *

The sky had turned violet, though it showed no stars, yet, and the moon had not risen. To the west, clouds gleamed rose and yellow, and a tower stood dark against them. Her face as expressionless as a mask, Jan slumped in her seat, and Elena lay beside her.

Not quite asleep, Colin thought. He pointed. "That belongs to the university. We'll reach it before full dark."

Jan looked, but showed no other response.

The train shuddered to a halt. Elena rubbed her eyes, Jan peered out, and feeling superstitious, Colin shut his mouth. An orange glow appeared behind the tower, like—a fire. Larger than a bonfire, but he could not judge.

Jan's breath hissed out. "You're a wizard. Can you get us there? Quickly?"

It was a fire; Jan, no doubt, could judge its nature to a hair's breadth. Colin eyed the light again, but answered truthfully, though he had to drag the words out of himself.

"Faster than the train."

Jan scooped up Elena. Colin looked at her. Bad enough to have to deal with the woman, but the baby as well?

"I am *not* leaving Elena here." Her face set. "Or anywhere else where she might be taken for a fire demon."

Colin studied her face for a moment. He could only manage faster than the train if they did not quarrel, and the fire, silent with distance, had to rage to bring that much light. He nodded and strode to the door, where he put one arm about her. She tilted her head to one side like a bird's, listening. Colin recited the spell, and flew into the night with her. His free arm extended, pointing the way for the spell. His enchantments held off the winds, he could not feel her weight or Elena's, and even the motion of their flight did not buffet them, but the warmth gave way to night air. Elena squawked indignantly.

* * *

It felt like a floor under their feet, and all else was engulfed in gloom; any other light was drowned by the blaze. Jan tightened her grip on Elena. The firelight grew closer, and heat rose toward them. Her tongue touched her lips. A large fire—larger than any she had seen at Firerock for many a year—and she did not know these woods.

"As close to the fire as possible," she said.

Smoke gusted into their faces, and Elena yelped. Colin swooped closer to the trees, beneath the smoke, where fierce orange lit up the gray billows from below, and into a gap, where beaten earth separated the trees. He flew along the path to the fire.

Elena leaned forward, wide-eyed.

Flames licked the air. Nothing moved inside them, not even a vaguely human form. Half a dozen figures surrounded the blaze. In long, blue, impractical robes, they chanted and moved their hands. Steam billowed up, almost blinding. A cold blast of air bent but did not quench the flames. Wind and water, thought Jan.

"I can hold Elena," Colin said.

"Not needed for this." Jan gestured with her free hand. Fledging blazes vanished like candle flames blown out, and sparks flew. Elena squealed and caught a handful. Jan chanted and gestured again. The fire contracted.

Some wizard cast a light spell. Under its blue glow mingling with firelight, casting odd shadows and discoloring all the scene, Jan walked over the half-burnt wood. Fire sank before her.

One young wizard wrung her hands. "It burned so *quickly*."

"Only fires started by firelings burn that swiftly," said Jan. The dying fire gilded faces all about. Or by firemasters, she thought. She met the wizards' gazes and said nothing of that.

The fire sighed out on its own ashes, leaving the icy blue the only illumination, and casting shadows sharp as knives on the trees about. Nothing looked natural by its light.

"But the fireling was gone by the time I arrived. I suspect by the time *you* arrived, or you would not talk of its quickness. I certainly could not have disposed of one that easily."

A gray-haired man puffed up like a bantam rooster. "We managed. If we could not manage, the whole university would have burned by now."

"You," said Colin, "can address your complaints to the king. No doubt, he will treat them with all due respect."

For a shocked moment, none of the wizards moved. Then, turning his face away, the gray-haired man grimaced. The light made his face look monstrous with its shadows.

"It's—" A young woman pushed back her hair. "She can stop it altogether. She's a firemaster." Her gaze drifted to Elena. "She no doubt brought—things to deal with fire—"

"Oh," said Jan icily. "What things are you speaking of?"

* * *

They walked along the path, back toward the train, instead of flying. Jan's golden light surrounded them, gilding the nearer trees and casting looming shadows from them on the trees behind. Elena chortled and opened her hand. "Spak." The spark glimmered and winked out. Elena pouted.

Colin looked at that little hand, thinking of more and more reasons why it might prove imprudent to have the child with them. He wished he had thought to ask the wizards to send word to the train that it could go on; he could have gotten the luggage once Jan, and Elena, were safely ensconced in their chambers, out of sight of both wizards and passengers.

Elena yawned and leaned on Jan's shoulder.

"Can anyone," Colin said, "do what Elena did? Anyone of any hair color?"

Jan hesitated. "No." The word dissolved into the silence before she added, "That we know of."

The train came into view ahead.

"Every firelord we ever heard of had red hair." She shrugged. Elena grumbled but did not stir again. "Not even we *encourage* infants to play in blazes. Perhaps even at Firerock, we have firelords among our number without our knowing of them. And out here—"

Her free hand swept the air, taking in the hills about, dismissively.

* * *

Stars speckled the sky, but as they reached the station, its snow-white light drowned them out. Travelers poured from the train, full of tales. Jan, looking not at all weary, walked off past the first crowd and looked about the station.

A light flared, down the train—red, flickering like flames in a wind—followed by panicky cries. Elena mumbled.

Jan stroked the girl's head and smiled, with a trace of malice. "Come," she said to him, and strode off. He followed, his eyes narrowed. The king had ordered that she come here, and ordered that he ease her way for her. . . .

At the baggage car, ghostly red fire danced about Jan's bags. Flames shot up to brush the roof—leaving no soot marks, and not heating the air. The porter gibbered: he had only gone to *move* the bags.

"You must have been careless." Jan walked over.

Colin's mouth twisted. The bags bore runes he should have noticed earlier, and one stood just a trifle open. Jan gestured, and the fires vanished faster than a blown-out candle flame, leaving the car dark. The bags, however vague, were clear enough; Colin took them up.

Out on the station, other travelers—none of them in wizards' robes—yielded the way and whispered, staring at them.

"Are they here to welcome us?" said Jan.

Colin followed her gaze to the blue-robed, dark-haired man, and a black-haired woman, wearing a gown rather than robes. "Yes. Martin—he visited Firerock once. For the king."

"I know," said Jan.

Then she had met him. That would explain why he had been chosen. "The woman is his wife Susannah."

Jan said nothing. The wizard and his wife came across the station.

Martin nodded, solemnly. "We met at Firerock—Jan."

Jan smiled, without its reaching her eyes. "My foster daughter, Elena."

Martin twitched, eyeing the drowsy child.

Colin hoped his message had reached them and spoke, quickly. "You may not remember me from among your students, sir."

Martin turned aside, quickly. "Among the students, no, young Colin, but we seldom lose students of promise, even if not *outstanding* promise, to family duties. It made you memorable." He smiled, coolly. "You have not met my wife, Susannah."

Colin bowed. Susannah nodded to him, though her gaze kept flickering back to Jan and the child.

"We prepared chambers for yourself, Mistress Jan, and for Master Colin." Martin eyed Elena.

"Add a child's bed to mine," said Jan.

"Didn't you get my message?" said Colin.

"Ah," said Martin, "something must have gone awry."

* * *

The university's servants moved quickly: a little bed, carved with stars and the moon, stood in the room when they reached it. Jan went to lay Elena down, but Colin held up a hand and dropped to one knee beside it, eyeing every inch.

He rose. "I have always found the servants here faithful and honest, but sometimes they think good service means not disturbing the wizards to ask whether a thing's enchanted."

Jan's mouth twisted, but she laid Elena down.

Colin looked about. The wizards had not stinted on their firemaster. The room, with its dark paneling and carpet, with bay windows that opened to the rose garden, was held for the university's finest guests. Noble guests would sleep here, and even royal ones, when they had them.

"Are you busy?" a voice caroled from the doorway. A dark-haired young woman, in dark blue robes, leaned in.

Jan eyed her fiercely.

Colin sighed. "Mistress Jan, my cousin Aliza. Aliza, we just arrived. The child is not the only tired one."

"I'd rather eat before I slept," said Jan, straightening. "If your cousin can tell the news—out of this room."

Aliza's mouth pursed. "A pity they sent Martin and Susannah to greet you. She miscarried last year."

"Oh," said Jan.

With the door closed, Aliza said, brightly, "Did you meet Susannah when Martin visited Firerock? He married on that journey, but I don't know whether before or after Firerock."

"Susannah and I are acquainted," said Jan, without a flicker.

Perhaps, thought Colin, Elena was not the only reason that another wizard should have greeted her.

* * *

The new risen moon cast some light on the path. Colin rubbed his eyes. Aliza had known little more than he had, but Jan had listened intently, and eating had taken longer after that. And he had to cross the university to reach the chancellor.

Who, at least, was still in his office. First the light in the window, and then when he had climbed in the stairs—

"Young Colin," the chancellor, Master Roger, said, urbanely. "A pleasure to see you again. I must apologize—the message made it to Master Martin's household, but not to his eyes—but the servants did their best on this notice—I trust your chambers have no flaw."

"None," said Colin. "It would be hard to return to the Students' Hall after this."

"More's the pity," said Master Roger, gesturing him to a chair. "I had heard that your sister married?"

Colin nodded as he sat.

"Then you are free of those duties your father's death brought you, and can return."

"Leave the king's service in the middle of this? I would think *you* would wish it least of all." He leaned forward. "Jan will need a nursemaid, too."

Master Roger's eyes narrowed.

"I doubt you want her to lug Elena about the university."

Master Roger shook his head. "How ridiculous, bringing so small a child. Surely the king expects—" Running out of words, he shook his head again.

"I think," said Colin, "that you might have guessed, in your years here, that mastery of magic does not require being a good judge of the ridiculous."

Master Roger's mouth twitched as if he had bitten something sour. "Warn this—Jan about our ways. I am sure she is unfamiliar with our need to study. She's a firemaster, after all."

He remembered her books. "I didn't know you had visited Firerock."

Master Roger looked puzzled. "I haven't."

Colin shrugged and stood. "Odd, then, that you know whether they study."

* * *

"This way." Wearing blue robes that reached the ground, Mistress Olivia swept toward a tower. Her iron-gray hair lay down her back in a single braid, and she gathered her skirts and climbed the stairs briskly, for all her lined face.

In a firemaster's yellow, Jan climbed after. Even if she removed her belt, the smock would barely fall to her knees. All about the building, wizards walked, wearing robes that *might* clear the ankles. Even the students did not wear them much shorter.

For a moment, she thought of demanding a wizard's robe for her skill at spellcraft—but her hair was enough to reveal her, she did not want to look ashamed, and the shorter smock *was* easier to run in. She didn't even have to lift her skirts on the stairs, as Mistress Olivia did.

On the roof, Mistress Olivia looked over the scene and turned rather pale.

"I have not been up here to see the damage for the last few. The fires all—they burn so quickly." She shook her head.

Jan leaned over the parapet. A pleasant breeze teased at her hair, carrying the scent of flowers. Green hills of trees and meadows spread before her, broken by soot-dark gaps like sores. Last night's blaze had left a scar, stark on the hillside, but smaller than others burned through the trees. Her mouth twitched. They could have coped, no doubt, last night.

Footsteps echoed on the stairs.

Mistress Olivia said, sharply, "What are you doing here, Perrin?"

A boyish voice said, "Bringing these." A coltish student burst through the doorway and held out a handful of blue flowers. "Look! Heaven-sents. Where the first fire burned -—it's *ablaze* with flowers." He could not keep the avidity from his voice.

"We must see that." Mistress Olivia eyed the flowers hungrily.

"A fierce fire, then, but—" Jan shrugged. "They're useful, but dangerous to rely on. I had to break myself of it."

Mistress Olive scowled. "Your tutor should have—"

"What, every student has a tutor? What luxury!" Jan left the parapet. Even plucked, the heaven-sents lent the air their fugitive, delicate smell. She scowled as a thought struck her. "Watch the flowers. If someone knew that heaven-sents grew where fires blazed, it is a reason to set fires."

Mistress Olivia paled. "Surely. . . ."

Jan smiled, knowing it would not reach her eyes. Mistress Olivia fell silent.

Perrin looked shocked, and then thoughtful, contemplating the blooms in his hand. "A ward spell," he said. "Ariadne's Labyrinth, or the Golden Walls, or the Seal of Stone—"

Jan felt hopeful. The wizards here might be of some use.

He looked at Jan. "Which ward would be best?"

It stung. "My tutor neglected *that*, too," she said.

* * *

Jan paced in her ever-so-fine room. Sunlight slanted through the window onto her path over the carpet. She wondered how many enchantments the room had, and how many were to keep her, or any other guest, harmless.

In the doorway, Colin said, "Do you need something?"

"A lesson in wards," said Jan, trying to keep her voice from harshness. "They expected me to know which was best for warding the heaven-sents." It had only taken Perrin moments to scurry off with his flowers, in fear of losing them to her; Mistress Olivia had, with some effort, come to a conclusion.

Colin closed the door, with only a breath of sound. "I heard they cast one."

"So they did. Ariadne's Labyrinth. Teach me it." Her hand formed a fist.

"That spell is convoluted," said Colin.

Her mouth twisted. She had, after all, watched them at every scar left by the fire; it hardly came as a surprise to her. "Worse than the Hieronymus Ward?"

He looked at her face for a minute, and gestured toward the table. "We can ward the candlestick."

* * *

Near noon, Jan cast the spell on candle and candlestick. She scowled at them both. Colin laughed, took her wrist, and drew her hand toward them. Their hands started to slip aside. Jan's scowl eased, but her forehead creased as she mapped out the ward, and how it shifted her hand away.

"And watch this." Colin dismissed the ward, lit the candle, and summoned it again. The candlelight looked watery and weak. "Things can't get out well either. Light's got the easiest job of it."

Jan smiled. Then—"You dismissed the ward."

He hesitated. "I saw you cast it. It is much harder if you do not."

"No doubt this university has many wizards who can cast hard spells. Even very hard ones. And heaven-sents can be quite valuable. So can other flowers that grow after fires. Useful for many kinds of magic. That they haven't sprouted *yet* doesn't—" Jan eyed the candle. "We don't even know that the wizards who cast the wards did not light the fire. Is there a way to see whether anyone tampers with the ward?"

She turned to face him. "Preferably without warning the wizard that it's there?"

* * *

Along the paths, through groves, nodding pale lilies in flowerbeds, and ivy-covered buildings, her yellow robe still drew glances. She wondered whether the wizards would ever grow used to it. It would take more than a few weeks, she did not doubt.

The path led into a grove.

"At least we can hide that we will watch," she muttered.

The trees ended, as abruptly as if a chunk of the woods had been scooped from the earth. Trees looked ridiculously elongated and sparse, their thin trunks reaching up to their few branches, high over-head. Their roots were charred, and the earth spread onward, black. Low leaves and petals sprouted on the sooty ground.

Ariadne's Labyrinth did not blur the blooms. Jan eyed them. If they had flowers that did not grow in Firerock—but she could make them out.

"The blue is heaven-sents. The white is star flowers, and love-waiting, that's the vine with rose red flowers. The little violet ones are little kings. That clump of red is—fire-bright."

"Fire-bright?" said Colin. "I've heard of that."

Jan straightened. She saw no places where sprigs had been broken off, or plants torn up; she had not seen them before, but then, watching the ward-casting had help her attention. "Few people, if any, went raiding before the ward." She tilted her head to one side. "And your spell?"

"It doesn't go on the ward," said Colin. "So no one will spy it there. It just watches."

Jan nodded. She watched, avidly, as Colin cast it, but at the end, she looked at her hands and sighed. She had learned so little, at her pitifully few books, without a tutor. "I think you will cast the spell every time we need it today."

Colin flexed his hands.

When they came out of the trees, in search of the next fire, a young woman awaited them. Her dark blue robes did not quite cover her worn cuffs.

"Mistress Jan?" Her eyes were dark, imploring.

Jan looked coldly at her. She would take the glances, because she had no choice, but she had no need to make herself a curiosity.

"Fourteen years ago—we were flooded—my father sent my brother to Firerock—they sent me to an aunt—" She stepped closer. "He was five."

For a moment, Jan's thoughts were utterly blank. She managed, somehow, to find words, and said, "What was his name?"

"Rob," said the woman, promptly.

"Rob," said Jan. "Fourteen years ago?" Wide-eyed, the woman blinked. "He's a firemaster now."

* * *

The evening breeze fluttered the curtains in Jan's chambers. The nursemaid, dismissed, scurried off. With a sigh, Jan sat in a chair. She bowed her head as if she would never rise from it.

"I don't think it's a fire spot."

Colin let his breath out. "We should send word to Lord Bertram of that—if you think it's sure enough."

"One fire at a time. Why haven't two firelings, or more, escaped? A swarm?" Jan leaned back. "They try it even at Firerock, where they know we wait for them."

Colin flinched at the thought; Jan could hardly fight two at once, and he had seen the wizards' efforts. Fetching more firemasters would be insanity. . . .

"But I don't think it's happenstance," Jan said. "Too many fires, too fierce."

Dishes clattered in the hall. Servants carried in soup and meat and salad and bread, all in fine china. When they closed the door, she started to serve herself and said, "It may be a fireling. It may be worse—a fire demon."

"No one's seen it," said Colin.

Her voice was solemn. "That is reason to suspect a fire demon. More cunning. It more than offsets the greater power, so that finding is harder, not easier." Jan took up her spoon. "Then there is how it came here—and there are the masters."

Colin, in the middle of ladling soup, stopped. The masters? They were no firemasters. "The masters wouldn't conjure up a fireling—let alone a fire demon."

"They *could*," said Jan. "If they had learned it."

Colin looked at his bowl and did not feel hungry.

"They have powerful reason to keep it secret," said Jan, "if they know such things. Even though they are not red-haired."

"Martin," said Colin, weakly. "He did go to Firerock."

"Susannah would not let him."

He took up his spoon. "You know them both."

Jan contemplated her bowl for a minute. Elena wailed, Jan's chair scrapped against the floor, and she ran. Colin tried to eat in her absence and wondered what, if anything, she would tell him after.

A minute later, Jan reappeared with Elena sobbing against her shoulder. "She—usually she doesn't have bad dreams," she said, apologetically. Elena hiccupped.

"She's far from home," said Colin. "In a strange place. And she does not know people here, as you know Susannah."

Jan sighed, but her voice was hard. "You'd best be able to keep a secret." She stroked Elena's hair.

"I am in the royal service," said Colin, his voice as hard. "The king does not opt for babble-mouths." As if she could confide anything in him as dangerous as whether a fire demon roamed about the university.

Jan's mouth twitched into a smile, which faded. "Susannah is my sister."

He blinked. The words seemed to make no sense at all.

"Also a firemaster—though she barely qualified. If you let it be known, she will kill you."

After a frozen moment, in which his thoughts refused to congeal, Colin's gaze went down, to her arms. "And Elena?"

Jan's smile was bitter. "I suspect. What other wizard could put Elena on my hearth? And Martin thought he was rescuing Susannah from the horrors of being a firemaster at Firerock, he would want to hide it, too. But I could not tell." She patted Elena's back again. "The tale of my sister's refusing to care for her red-haired child would spread all over Firerock."

Colin's mouth twisted. "And they still wouldn't believe you. That she is not your child."

"That too, but also, someone would tell Elena, eventually." Her mouth set in harsh lines.

Colin dragged his breath in. "Could *Susannah* have—"

Jan shook her head. "She hates firemastery. And never learned enough to do this." She carried Elena back to her bed, and Colin pondered. She sounded quite definite in the matter.

When Jan emerged again, he said, "What's the first spell you learn as a firemaster?"

"You know it. You have to be close to cast it—these fires were not cast by it, or someone would have seen."

"You forget, Mistress Jan," said Colin. "There is no *need* for wizards to be seen. No matter how close."

After a minute, Jan muttered, "Susannah would be too afraid of being found out." She raised her voice. "The second spell would help. If they are not firelords, firemasters must learn to protect themselves from fire."

Colin looked at the darkening sky outside. "It might be best to teach me that spell." Scarlet was giving way to purple and crimson, and he let out his breath. Jan had a point. He would fail in his duty if he did not help her with it. "In the morning, we can consider what masters are most likely."

* * *

With mist in the air, the dawn was gray, but Jan moved in her chambers. Colin came in.

Elena, chortling, hurled across the floor. Colin snatched her before she reached the door, and she squealed with glee. He looked at her smile for a moment before he realized that she had not wanted the doorway. He smiled back, surprising himself.

"The nursemaid will be here soon," said Jan.

Colin handed the bright-eyed Elena over. "I can order a search of the masters' houses, if we would find anything, but it would warn our culprit to start."

Jan nodded.

"They're all here—there haven't been any changes recently—except Gerard, and he died."

"Oh." The word was very hard. Colin, for a moment, found it hard to breathe. He had agreed to consider, he reminded himself, but he could put no conviction in that thought.

Elena said, "Mama?" but Jan still did not stir.

"When did he die?" she said.

"A fortnight before the fires started." Which, he thought, his stomach lurching, might not mean a thing.

Jan looked as if she stared through the walls.

"Gerard was deeply respected," said Colin.

"And, he's dead." Jan straightened. "Can you get the keys secretly? I will take Elena for a walk. That might keep tongues from wagging for a moment or two." Her mouth twitched. "Maybe even *three*."

* * *

Tucked away in a tree-filled square, Gerard's rooms were on the ground floor. Thick ivy, darkly green, hid the stones, and the eaves shadowed the door.

Colin tried the key. It turned easily in the lock. He fought to keep from glancing about; it would only attract attention, but that thought did not calm his heart. He shoved the door open.

Through the diamond-paned windows, the light was tinted green by the ivy leaves. The ashes had long been raked from the cold hearth, and dust lay like a thin gray veil, utterly smooth, over the tables, bookcases, chairs—and all the books.

"Looks like most wizards' rooms," said Colin.

Jan's mouth tightened, eying the stacks. Colin looked away, feeling guilty. He had seen her books. She had fewer than were in the smallest stack, and she could borrow from neither other wizards nor a library.

Jan put Elena down, handed the baby some brightly colored blocks, and turned to the books.

"The works of Hieronymus," she said. "That one I know taught him no firemastery."

They worked through piles. Every now and again, they put aside a book whose title hinted at things that could mean firemastery, or Colin told Jan that a book strange to her was a standard text, or they glanced through a few pages to recognize a book's intent.

Then her hands fell on—"A Book of Flames," she announced, and leafed through it. "A spell to protect from fire—you have no need to read this one, after last night, Colin."

His mouth tightened, and he searched the books near that one. "The Fiery Art," he said. Jan nodded but did not look up. He searched on and put aside four others for Jan to inspect.

Under the table, Elena cooed.

Jan scrambled after the girl. A minute later, she emerged, with Elena under one arm, and her other hand holding a half-melted glass jar. A *thick* glass jar, and large, nearly half Elena's size. Only a fiercely hot fire could have melted it like that.

Colin felt very cold. To distract himself, he raised a hand and cast a spell. All about, a fiery veil appeared, a glow more uniform than the dust.

"Fiah!" shouted Elena. Her fingers slid through the glow, and she pouted.

Colin lowered his hand. The light vanished, but his heart hammered like a drum. He forced the words from his mouth. "The room is protected from firemastery, by the spell you taught me. He must have—the spell I cast, it discerns whether any spell you know is in action."

Jan looked at the bland dust and books. "I have to learn that spell."

"It's advanced work," said Colin.

"Like the Hieronymus ward?" Jan put down the jar. "This, and those books, have to get back to my chambers unseen." Her mouth smiled mirthlessly. Her eyes were cold. "You said it could be done."

* * *

The nursemaid glanced at both books and jar. Jan held out Elena to her. Pale, she snatched the girl and vanished into the back room.

With the books on the table, Jan took up a book. She would have to read through every one, and every page of every one, no doubt, and find the knowledge on the last page of the last book.

Colin, his expression diffident, took up another. For a moment, she wondered if he could recognize firemastery on the page, but if not, he would hardly do any harm.

The door burst open, thudding against the wall. Jan jumped, and her heart hammered. Mistress Olivia glared at them both.

"You," said Mistress Olivia. "What were you thinking? Treating a master wizard like a common thief?"

Jan forced her breath in and out. Her heart calmed.

Colin surged to his feet. "No wonder you wanted me as a student again—subject to your authority. I am—we are—in the king's service, and we do not answer to you."

Jan's mouth pursed as she looked at them both. Colin seemed to handle it well enough.

"Stealing a master's books." Mistress Olivia strode closer. "Like a common thief. And for what? Firemasters do not study like true wizards."

Jan's snort of laughter was so derisive that Mistress Olivia fell silent, her mouth gaping.

"A common thief, he wasn't. A common arsonist, now—" Jan produced the jar. "Can you explain this, Mistress Olivia?"

Mistress Olivia glared at her. Elena sobbed. Jan put the jar on the table and left for the nursery. The nursemaid helplessly sputtered about Elena, as if too afraid to pick her up. Jan sighed and returned with the child against her shoulder.

Mistress   Olivia   still   glared   at   the   jar. "Where—did—you—find—that?"

"At Master Gerard's. Elena found it—hidden as if dangerous."

Mistress Olivia's lip curled. "Your little firelord? I dare say she melted it!"

Jan sighed. "It was *already cool*." Elena hiccupped, and Jan patted her back and wondered whether Mistress Olivia would believe that mattered. Merely not investigating the fires themselves did not mean that the master wizards thought they could not pronounce whether a thing was firemastery.

Mistress Olivia opened her mouth when footsteps rang down the hall.

Aliza burst in. "There's another fire—over the hill this time."

"Which way?" Colin surged to his feet.

"I'll show you," said Aliza.

Jan brushed by Mistress Olivia. Colin, hurrying after, glanced at Elena, whose face was still wet.

Jan did not seem to glanced sideways, but she said, "Who shall I leave her with? Mistress Olivia?"

As soon as they stepped outside, they did not need a guide: smoke billowed over the hilltops. Jan took a step forward, but Colin grabbed her wrist. A moment later, with his arm about her, they flew over the hillside.

Elena shouted with glee, her face still wet but her eyes clear.

"She's going to be spoiled," muttered Colin, and Jan laughed.

Moments later, they flew over a small village. Peasants drove beasts and geese away from the blaze, and the smoke billowed ever more thickly. Colin sank, below the heated air and smoke.

Among the flames, a woman walked: her hair as fiery red as Jan's, her face as yellow as a candle flame, her dress a dark yellow, flickering and forming like a fire in the wind.

Jan's heart hammered. The reason behind Firerock, why the red-haired children were sent there—the true fire demon.

Her feet were not well formed enough that they could be said to be bare or shod, the only sign that she sprang from the flames. She looked up—at Jan and not Colin. Her eyes were as black as coal, and her smile held no mirth.

Colin plummeted to the earth. "Give me Elena."

Jan hesitated for only a moment; then, unencumbered, she ran forward. The thing smiled, showing a white-hot mouth. Jan raised her hands and cast her strongest protection spell on herself. The fire demon's smile widened farther than a human's mouth could move, and her hands spread. Fire flew out like wings, and peasants screamed behind Jan.

She could do nothing if she let the fire demon burn her alive.

"So—" The fire demon stretched out a hand. "The three of you came. Then the one of you comes—"

For a moment, Jan's breath hurt. She prayed that Colin could cast the protection spell swiftly enough, and realized that he needed to. Then she straightened. She had a better defense than that, the fire demon could not attack Colin while defending against *her*. Her hands flew in an encompassing spell.

"You think to trap *me*?" The fire demon's flames surged out, fiercely orange. Jan braced herself. The flames beat against the spell and shot upward.

The fire demon glared. "I will leap over your little spells and burn you to cinders."

"You will not." Jan cast another spell. The demon's fires blazed more fiercely. The fire demon roared like a burning house. She scowled in thought, and Jan strengthened the spell, before the fire demon realized. Sweat beaded on her face, and the encompassing spell was strained, but the fire demon had to burn something, and when she did, it was consumed.

"*YOU* will not!" screamed the fire demon.

The air seared with heat, but she breathed in and out and did not choke. As long as it was not smoke. . . Jan bent her attention on keeping the fire blazing. Minute after minute, it raged. Then it sputtered for the lack of anything to burn. Jan set her jaw. Half done. All done would be better.

The fire demon sank and sank, to lie like a beleaguered maiden on charred black earth. Jan watched for a minute. When the fire demon did not stir, she cast swift, sharp spells. The demon vanished like a blown-out candle.

A minute later, she let her breath out. The breeze had already blown away the fierce heat. She walked toward the villagers.

They had surrounded someone small.

"You—" spat an old man, and Jan heard the sound of a hand striking flesh. She ran forward.

The old man turned toward her, his lips pulling back from his teeth. The peasants parted enough that Jan could see an auburn-haired boy in their midst, but the man was bent on her.

"You! How many monsters are there?" said the old man.

Colin's voice rose. "How many do you think?"

He stalked toward them, with Elena in his arms, with a fiery glow all about him. Shrieking, the peasants fled.

Jan ran to snatch the boy and hold him, despite his terrified glances at Colin; then she could stand and stare at the glow. She would have a hard time mastering fire so.

"I—" she said. "I did not know you knew such a spell."

"It's a seeming," said Colin. "Do you know a spell that can do it in truth?" He grinned.

* * *

At the railway station, the porter looked resigned as Jan handed over the boy, mute and still bruised, to go to Firerock. She walked back up the slope to where Colin waited on the grass, and Elena gamboled.

"I'd go myself, if I could," she said, "but wizards need to go to Firerock and learn firemastery. This was too dangerous. Which means I need to persuade them." She took Elena's hand.

"They should send a master to tutor children at Firerock, as well," said Colin. "A shame to lose *promising* students because they are firemasters as well."

Jan glanced at him.

"It might take some time to send one, but there are Gerard's books. Many *look* like works on wizardry, but he would have hidden any knowledge. At Firerock, you can peruse them to look for it, and be sure to take enough time to be certain. I am sure the king will override the wizards, if they try to object to sending them."

They walked under an arched gate, into the university.

"To ensure that they are not firemastery, you might have to learn and cast them." He bowed. "I would be happy to help."

Jan smiled, and curtsied in return. "That would make me happy."

Ripening Gold

The roses bloomed behind her and filled the air with sweetness. Rosette, kneeling on the flagstones, could not look at them. Coin by coin, she turned each one and made sure it sat in the sun. By now, they were not so much lead as *metallic* and even showing signs of gold. Still, they needed many a day of sunning to become gold. Many a day inching sideways on her knees. Many days had passed, and more were to come.

She turned another.

Her father Ruggerio had sworn and raged when he had to leave, as if inheriting a title were a plot against him, and he threatened to raze her roses if she did not meticulously carry this out. Sometimes, she wondered what he would do to replace the roses' protective enchantments, but every day, she turned the coins over and shifted them into the sun from shadows.

She used it to dawdle, Rosette told herself. She turned the last coin, stood, and walked through the archway into her golden garden. It held southern roses in every shade of yellow that roses could bear, with buzzing bees and golden butterflies—perhaps golden from the solar enchantments so heavy on the cottage. Sometimes she wondered about her own golden coloring, both her golden hair and her so easily but lightly tanned skin. Neither of her parents, whether Ruggerio, or Gloriana before her death, had given her a straight answer.

The door inside appeared ahead of her like a dark cave, and she stopped. She knew her routine; she had taken advantage of her father's absence to make it as regular as sunrise and sunset. Go in. Write to Justin. If Saturday, mail the week's letter off. Commence her studies. Except—except that since her father inherited that title (and been summoned to court), Justin had never written back.

Rosette had been more relieved by the absence forced on her father than she had cared about her new state. But now—she walked in, slowly—had Justin decided a noblewoman was of no interest to him? Found another sweetheart? She had no grounds for complaint if he had, she thought forlornly. She had put him off, told him that she had to finish the studies laid out in her mother's will before she could even think of marrying. It was the condition of her being her mother's heiress. (And it had been Justin who had alerted her to the will. He had not said, when she refused him, that he wished he had kept his silence. But he might have come to wish it.)

She reached her study, and stood in the doorway.

Those very studies could aid her now. She would *know*, even know the worst, and she should stop wavering and do the enchantment.

She opened the book. The section was not where she had been studying, but she did have to master it sooner or later. She laid the rose carefully aside, and began to read.

Footsteps sounded on the walkway. Between masses of goldenrod, old Master Thomas walked up, with a letter in hand. Her heart drummed in her chest, no faster than usual, but harder.

They received letters, she reminded herself. One reason her father had left her here was to ensure she dealt with any from the magistrate or merchants. This could be something of no importance at all.

Her heart still did not calm as she crossed the floor and opened the door before he knocked. She glanced down, and saw a royal seal.

Her heart settled at once. She did not need to see the direction to know it was not Justin's.

Master Thomas lifted the letter and smiled mischievously. "What's the point of your father gallivanting off to court? When the king has to send letters here?"

"Who knows the thoughts of kings?" said Rosette. "It must content us lowly ones to serve them fittingly."

Master Thomas's smile twisted ironically. He handed over the letter—addressed, of course, to her, not her father—and sauntered off. She closed the door before breaking the seal.

In the king's name, it directed Mistress Rosette to aid her father's work in all things necessary that he might serve the king and the kingdom, and gave her authority to demand aid from all royal officials for those ends, including creating a package for her father of all objects and materials he might need in his new work. It included a list.

She looked up and at the gargoyle sitting by the stairs. "Every one of these, my father could buy at Kingston. There is no need for me to send them."

The gargoyle shrugged. "True, inscrutable are the thoughts of kings." It turned toward the stairs. "No doubt you'll manage to get it off, in your own sweet time."

She bore the letter back to her study. The rose would not keep, and that package would.

Fill a golden bowl with pure water. Float the rose in it. Cast the enchantment and watch it point north. Refine it to point at Justin. Elaborate it—she scowled and reread the direction to be certain—to discern problem.

The rose withered in the water. Parts of it turned black as pitch, as if it had rotted in the moments it lay there.

Rosette stared at it. After a moment, she realized she had grabbed the table to steady herself. She forced her breath in and out and whirled back to the room. The hearth was closest. She took two steps to reach it and sat on the stone.

And there she sat, shuddering. She barely noticed the hardness. Light from the windows inched across the floor.

If he were dead, it would have turned all black, she told herself. She needed to read. . . .

The book spoke of what the problems could be, from the signs of the rose. But it spoke only of black for the dead, not even the dying, as well as insisting that the rose would be entirely black if so.

She closed the book slowly. She had wanted to complete her studies.

* * *

"Eh, what are you doing here?" said the gargoyle.

Rosette looked about her father's study, picked out the crystal ball, and walked over.

"And—" Its voice grew sharper. "—what are you doing with that? That's your father's pride and joy. And it can't be on the list."

"Doing what my father gave me leave to do by leaving me in charge of the cottage," said Rosette coldly. "If he wanted you to control what lay in his study, he would have left *you* in charge. And the letter would have been addressed to you, about the package."

She did not pick up the crystal. The stand kept it in place, and the crystal was so powerful that it was simple to cast the enchantment. It was like looking through a window of the finest glass. . . .

Out on a ghastly swamp. Trees hung over all, heavy with moss, blocking out the sun. She thought most of them were dead, their branches stark in themselves but overgrown with hanging moss. Then, the moss looked rather dead, as well. Stretches of water reflected nothing, and revealed nothing of their depths in their darkness. All of them pools, without a hint of motion in them. Not so much as a dragonfly skimmed the waters. Between, the stretches of earth were overgrown with dark green, but the plants were sprawled on the earth. A few flowers blossomed there—midnight blue or royal purple blooms. Or had they darkened in death?

On a patch of higher ground, still muddy, a company of soldiers spread about. She frowned for a moment, aware that some enchantment guarded them, but unable to work out what they had wrought and maintained.

She glanced at the men again, trying to make them out. She could not bring it much closer, not enough to see faces, but patches of black on them held her eye. As black as the rose had turned—and like the rose, they were not entirely turned. They still held the enchantment against this wizardry.

This necromancy, she thought, feeling cold. And if the enchantment failed. . . .

Or rather, when. No enchantment lasted forever while the necromancy ate at it, and this one was not strong enough to destroy the necromancy.

Rosette did not even notice when her own enchantment failed, and the crystal returns to its colorless state.

"Huh." The gargoyle hopped on the desk and peered into her face, its enormous eyes coming within inches of hers. "What sort of daughter sits about when her father's great work sits in the shade, when it needs to sit in the sun?"

Devil take my father's great work, she thought. I need to—I need to—

I need to hunt through my father's books to find what I can do, which means I need to keep him content and far from here. She surged to her feet, nearly knocking the gargoyle over, and ignored its objections as she ran down the stairs to the courtyard.

* * *

She considered, as she packed up the supplies, that her father might have sent the list to stall, not wishing to work for the king.

As was his duty, she told herself virtuously.

She looked out the window at the flower clock. Morning glory still in yellow bloom, and the noon flowers, white and yellow and blue, still opening in glorious color. If the package would not leave until tomorrow, still a dutiful daughter would bring it today, as early as she could.

Especially when she did not have to worry about money. The king himself had authorized her prerogative to send it as a royal package. (All right, the clerk signing his name and affixing the seal—but still she did not need to wonder.)

* * *

The gargoyle glared at her. Stacks of books everywhere, and she was quite certain she could never put them back where she had found them.

The sunset outside was flaming orange and red as she reached for another.

"Mistress," said a voice from the doorway. The gryphon-shaped gargoyle sat there. "Mistress Gloriana always said that failing to eat meant folly in studies."

Rosette groaned. Yes, she had to eat. And she had to sleep as well. She looked at the book. She had read much of necromancy in the last hours, but nothing of use. It seemed to bring out the romancers, telling legends of dragons and dwarves. And roses. But none of the rose stories were so practical as the enchantments she learned from her mother's book. And certainly not so detailed enough that she could work out the enchantments.

Rosette scowled. Perhaps she had chosen the wrong book. She stood up. The gryphon had been opening its beak to address her again, but closed it with a satisfied look on its eagle face. She followed it into the kitchen, but her thoughts beat about the same loop: her mother's will had required her to learn one of a score of books before she married, to claim her inheritance. If she had chosen one of the others, she might have mastered enchantments that would let her save Justin and his fellows.

A short, bitter bark of laughter escaped her.

"Mistress?" said the gryphon.

"It's nothing," said Rosette. And it was, indeed, nothing. The enchantments were reliable. That scene had showed her where Justin was; it did not matter that she had not actually *seen* him.

If he were not there, it would still be her duty, as a subject of the king, to deploy her enchantments against this necromancy. She was, after all, the daughter and heiress of a margrave.

For a moment, as the gryphon pushed a plate before her, she pondered why enchanters were always made margraves, rather than barons or any other title. Though it was clear enough why the title passed only to those who mastered enchantments.

The gryphon cleared its throat. She ate.

*　*　*

Rosette yawned. The little globe of sunlight, stolen from the skies above the grip of night, was not bright enough to delude her into thinking that it was day.

Which was just as well. She might miss something vital while she read.

At least this book was practical work, not fancy tales. (She was filled with astonishment at how many of her father's works were filled with such tales. Did he merely fill up the shelves to make himself look more learned?)

She yawned again and looked back down.

The virtue of alchemical gold, ripened by the sun, is to bring about with like sympathy, the restoring of unsound things to soundness.

She blinked, tried to read it again, and then carefully reached for a bookmark. She would read it in the morning. With her wits about her.

Her mouth twitched.

By sunlight.

*　*　*

By sunlight, she took careful clippings of her roses. Her precious roses, which her father might raze. . . .

This was more important. She laid another clipping in her satchel, with its enchantments to keep them preserved. Three from each rose bush, because they would not be easy to replace. Even with these it would take years to grow back her garden. . . she forced her breath in and out.

Behind her back, the coins still lay in the sun. She had cast an enchantment to be certain they were not on the brink of full ripeness, which would seal the virtue in—and please her father.

This, she told herself, would please the king. She might end up a margravine in her own right.

She looked at the house. The king might tell her father to let her have what she inherited, but he could not order her father to let her ever set foot in his house again. And her father could root up and utterly destroy the roses as he threatened before the king ever had word of what he did.

If, she reminded herself, she carried out her plan. If she failed, Justin would die, many other men would die, necromancy would extend its dark blight, but she could return to her father's house, and he would never know how close his treasured gold came to vanishing.

Assuming that she lived.

She went to gather the coins, and seal them away with enchantments, to ripen no more.

* * *

Her pouch heavy with coins that were very nearly but not quite gold, Rosette put the key to the lock and closed the gate as well as all the doors.

She put the key away, and ignored the curious glances as she walked down the street. Justin had lived in his parents' house, three streets over. A narrow, tall one, in a row of houses, with a tiny garden in the back. Which, perhaps, was more than they needed, they were gone so often in the king's service.

She walked up to the bright blue door, and used the knocker. A commonplace knocker, her mother would have said. Not even showing a sign that enchanters lived within.

It knocked soundly, better than the knocker with the solar face at her home.

Women walked by with baskets of bread and carrots on their arms. Carts rattled by, some with firewood, others with barrels of wine, still others with loads in chests and bales. Her tongue touched her lips. How long could she wait? She stared at the windows, lead-lined diamond panels that mirrored back the street. Birds flitted down the street and up into the air again. She swallowed. She did not know that his parents were here, at that. Sticking to her studies kept her from the gossip.

The door opened, and Magnus looked out. A tall, strongly built man, with dark hair and eyes—Justin was of his height, but had his mother's tawny coloring—his face a mask, he looked her up and down. She swallowed and tried not to peer into the hall. No one moved; Helen might not be about.

His dark eyes came back to her face. She did not need to read an expression to know that he knew she was going on a journey.

"What brings you here, Mistress Rosette?"

"Why, your son, Master Magnus," she said. And hoped it did not sound brittle to him.

He muttered something taking her long enough.

"Silence is harder to interpret than news," said Rosette. "But I know now, and I wish to help him."

His face twisted, but he smoothed it out again in moments. "There is nothing you can do to help," he said, sternly. "You do not know the battlefield as I do, Mistress Rosette. You do not know how little your little sunlit enchantments can do. Go back to your gardens and your books. That's the sort of enchantment that suits your skills."

"The king does not think so." Rosette produced the letter. "The king thinks that my father's enchantments should be used to help the kingdom."

Magnus reached out to take it. Rosette lowered her hand and looked pointedly at the hallway behind.

After a moment, he stepped back and let her into the white-washed hall. She caught a glimpse of a mirror at the end—was she really that pale?—but turned to him and handed over the letter.

Minutes later, he scowled. "You play at games, Mistress Rosette." He lowered it. "Only a malleable reading would get you within a league of my son, and it would give you only mundane aid."

She straightened. "Then, sir, if you would of your courtesy tell me where I might find someone who would read it in a malleable manner, I would be grateful. If not, I shall have to just inquire for such a one. I would think that more haste would be prudent."

His mouth twitched.

* * *

The sky lowered. The tents ahead were vague shadows beneath the clouds.

Magnus greeted the sentry with a "Hullo!" and spoke to him in a low voice. When a messenger went off to the general, he came back to Rosette.

"Do soldiers all greet each other like mountaineers shouting across a crevice?" said Rosette.

"Oh yes," said Magnus. He glanced sideways at her. "You probably ought to do it too, since you're coming to fight."

Rosette opened her mouth and shut it.

* * *

She pulled her hood closer. The sky, from horizon to horizon, was covered with thick, leaden clouds. Every now and again, thunder rumbled. From the grumbles about, it would rain. Sometime today. For hours. As it had for weeks.

The coins, still not quite gold, weighed heavily in her bag. The satchel with the rose clippings hung over her shoulder. Ahead of her, the swamp spread, and her mouth tightened. The crystal had been clear, but it had not been large, and she had not seen clearly.

The trees had indeed died already. The moss, dying, hung on leafless boughs. The grass lay flattened, and the flowers she had seen were dying on the stem. Darkling blight lay everywhere on the plants.

The black across the leaves did not look much different than it had on the men. She shivered. At least, if what she remembered from the crystal had been faithful.

"Huh."

She turned to look at the officer eyeing her.

"Thinking that good clothes to wear to a battlefield?"

"I beg your pardon," said Rosette, crisply. "Next time, I will dillydally, fussing about the *proper* attire like a courtier at court—and a courtier seeking royal favor—when I have crucial knowledge for the battlefield."

A huff of laughter came from behind the officer, and she realized that the general himself stood there. She nodded rather than try either "Good morning" or "Hullo."

"How crucial can it be?" said the general. "We can't let you within a league of it."

"Then you have grave difficulties," said Rosette. "The only thing holding it back is the enchantments the men managed to cast before the necromancer trapped them. And though they are heroic work, they can not last forever. They will break."

Silence fell. There was not so much as a breeze or birdsong about her. She fought down the impulse to babble on about how the necromancy would get out.

The general's voice sounded half a snarl when he spoke. "If you have some fancy way to protect yourself, to get near enough to do some good—"

Rosette swallowed. The bag of rose slips was heavy on her shoulder.

* * *

A league was an exaggeration. It could not have been a sixth of the way to the islet where they were trapped.

Rosette swallowed and lowered her two bags to open them. Perhaps she could save some slips, it would not take all of the roses to reach the men. . . but she pulled out a coin and one of the roses, knelt to put the rose into the dead mire, and began the enchantment. Golden sunlight poured from the metal, and the rose began to grow, drinking up water and spread its branches toward the islet.

The coin turned back into lead.

As soon as the footing would let her, she pressed on. She needed haste. She had to get to the islet with coins enough that she could free the men, and so could not use them all on the roses. She put down down another rose, and then another.

Half way there, a glance back showed how far she had left the soldiers behind. They stared in silence and did not follow. She gulped. Wise of them. She needed to make sure that she could get back in time. Such hastily grown roses—she hesitated, and tested one. Quick growth would mean weakness and failure.

The rose bushes stood as stout as any in her father's garden. She blinked. The solar enchantment must have—

She had no time to theorize, she told herself. She put down yet another rose and followed the path she made. Rose petals showered on her as she went under the last rose bushes and up onto the islet.

The first man she saw lying there was a stranger to her; that was clear even with his face utterly obscured with the blight. She held the latest coin and pulled out more of the sunlight for the enchantment. The blight pulled back, revealing a face rugged and ordinary.

The coin ran out before she finished. Grimacing, Rosette pulled out another. A minute later, the man started to stir. She did not give him time to speak, hurrying onward.

She went from soldier to soldier, pulling the blight away, taking care not to slop the light about. The grass and the trees and the flowers did not need to be restored. Soldier after soldier stirred, and coin after coin vanished from her pouch.

Until finally, she was looking about, her heart drumming. She was down to her last coin, she could not see another soldier, and she had not found Justin.

A cold thought reminded this was her duty to king and kingdom, even if she were too late. She told it that it was her duty to king and kingdom to save every soldier, if she could.

"Justin," she said. "Where is Justin?"

"He's dead," said the captain, heavily.

Her heart hammered.

"It was heroic, he broke the first attack, and we would have never managed without it."

She forced herself to swallow. "Where?" she said, choking the word out.

"You needn't—"

"*Where?*"

He pointed.

She darted past the tree and nearly stumbled on Justin where he lay, unrecognizable from the blight. She dropped to her knees and squeezed the light out. Sunlight poured over him, and the blight eased back, slowly, slowly, until she could just recognize his face, and the coin was giving up its last.

She swallowed, hard. He still did not stir.

A petal fell down from her hair. She shook her head. More of the petals fell. The petals she had conjured with the sunlight, that she could have used here—the newly formed petals—

She reached down and forced the sunlight out of them, into Justin. The petals turned to wisps and then to dust, and she could only kneel beside him. He did not breathe, and neither did she. She combed her hair, and a last petal fell. She added its tiny gleam to the sum.

Slowly, as the glimmer faded, his chest rose. Then it fell again, and she bit her lip until he breathed again. The last of the blight eased from his body.

Justin opened his eyes.

For a moment, they seemed blank. Then they focused on her, and he smiled.

"Hullo," he said softly.

Rosette smiled back. "Hullo."

Queen Shulamith's Ball

A ball, a ball, Queen Shulamith would hold a ball. . . .

Throughout the city, down every street, sibilant rumors ran. Even the birds, drab or jewel-bright, twittered of the rumors in their nests, tucked in the crevices of gray stone carvings. On a street corner, a drunkard, in tatters of green and scarlet, waved his bottle in air and—with marginal coherence—declaimed on how the ball would change the lives of many within the city before he slumped against the lamppost, and then to the pavement, to snore. And every passerby, eyeing the gray stone of the houses on her street, was sure to pick out hers.

When, in the gray early morning, Queen Shulamith appeared on her front steps, between the pillars, her violet gown swept the stone. She wore no jewelry, but her black hair, braided, wound about her head like a crown. The crowd shifted as people glanced and murmured. A sour old peddler, unable to hawk his apples when no one looked at him, muttered that it wasn't as if the city didn't have a ball, or two or three, every week. The queen paid none of them the least heed as she spoke with servants.

Two little girls walked in their white pinafores and blue dresses—black-haired Carol and little fair-haired Nina—to Queen Hesione's refined school, founded after her husband drank the money from selling their crowns. They passed the peddler without buying an apple and whispered of Queen Shulamith. She was only a queen, after all, like Queen Hesione, or the aunt of one girl and the second cousin of the other. She had to be an exile, too, or she would be making treaties and negotiating alliances. For all her grand house, if she lost her money, Queen Shulamith might open a school, too. . . .

Holding hands, they ran up the stairs.

"Are you?" piped Nina, quieting the square. "Are you really holding a ball?"

Queen Shulamith smiled down at the girls. "Yes." Her voice carried over the square in a sudden stillness. "Young people must meet, after all. Young or old, we must amuse themselves, and tongues and hearts of flint must find some way to gather as well, or they will risk their health, wading through poor weather to gossip, and then they would die in their sins."

Baffled, but remembering their etiquette classes, the girls thanked her. They forgot everything else as they scrambled down the steps, but they assured everyone they met that Queen Shulamith would give a ball, until they climbed the stairs to the school and did not quite tell all the other girls before Queen Hesione hushed them and sent them to their classes. One little girl, in the corridors, said, scornfully, that they would have been wiser to ask about the queen's magical mirrors, everyone knew Queen Shulamith had magical mirrors in her house like nothing else in the city, and balls were every day. The other girls resolved to listen at the windows.

Even with the windows open, little drifted in, as people talked of this and that, about the river ribbons and the scandal about Lady Rose-Lily, and only now and again about Queen Shulamith—and Queen Hesione or another teacher called them back to dreariness of history or mathematics or embroidery, while every other tongue in the square carried the tale further, and the news passed on from mouth to mouth, engulfing the city like a tide. Girls just old enough to attend exulted in their age, and lorded over their younger sisters, who pouted that a few years—or months, or weeks—cut them off from such a marvel, when Queen Shulamith never held balls. Maidens old enough to be sure murmured about the promise, and peril, of her famed magical mirrors, and whether it was wise to attend a ball where unknown magic could affect them all. Shopkeepers, whether selling lace or cloth or feathers, or any frippery at all, calculated their prices and how much more they could sell for such a novelty; the fancy, attending the ball, would not let themselves wear only such finery as would do for a more common ball,

given by a more ordinary queen. Hostesses made haughty, cutting re-
marks about how she had obviously chosen the time to undercut their
own balls.

Out on a street corner, a dark-haired young woman in a flame-col-
ored gown danced with a bear. A scattering of coins fell. After each
dance, she gathered coins and turned to dance again, except when she
and the bear moved to a new corner. In her pirouettes, Gemma half-
heard the whispers about where she came from, and those of other
things. Queen Shulamith's ball caught her ear, as much as she dared listen. One girl, pouting, told her mother she would never get to attend
so fine a ball, and Gemma pirouetted outward, into her path.

"I might be at the ball, to dance and amuse the guests—" Her voice
rang over the cobblestones. "—but you can watch me dancing here before then."

The mother hustled the girl onward. Gemma, a half-smile on her
lips, turned back to dancing with the bear. A delivery boy shook his
head and went on. At the Golden Bird bakery, he joined with a cooking
girl to ape those fancy dancers in pirouettes that sent flour flying.
Laughter and applause engulfed them, until the baker shouted them
back to work. The delivery boy took the next batch and fled out the
door, down a street full of stalls.

An old man, smoking his pipe before his stall of pots, watched the
boy run. He would not speak first of the ball himself, but whenever a
customer, or a passerby, spoke of it, he took out the pipe to pronounce
that this ball would produce many a change in the city, mark his words
and watch them happen.

Even on High Street, where all the narrow but high houses rose ten
and twelve floors, in a parlor on a seventh floor, when they gathered in
the morning (just before noon), the gossiping women mentioned the
ball before Alixandre said that a knight's wife had given birth to a fox.
"Or so it was said."

"Really," said Blanca, lifting her tea cup, "the lower orders are getting entirely above themselves."

"I blame Queen Lenore," said Ida. "She gave them all the idea—giving birth to a bear prince!" She waved her hand over the tea set, with its painted pink rosebuds and its inlay of gold. "And then everyone from the duchesses down to the wives of knights took it up."

"Let us just hope that it doesn't get down into the commoners." Alixandre went to pour herself another cup of tea. "Who knows what they would do? Cats from a merchant's wife?"

"Worse," said Blanca, "it might get out to the peasants, and we will hear of rabbit children."

Alixandre's mouth twisted. "I suppose we will have to wait and see about that—one never can tell—why, I even heard that there is to be another invasion of the city!"

"Really?" said Ida.

"Really," said Alixandre. "One would think they never learned."

"Some people do," said Blanca. "They come to the city nonetheless, for all the rumors." She pointed out the window. For the first time since they gathered, the other women looked out. It took some effort, with the parlor's height, and the morning leaving the street engulfed in shadow, but still they could see the carriage down on the ribbon of a street.

Ida eyed the sky and sipped some tea. "Early to arrive. One wonders when they left, and where they spent the night."

Beneath her eye, the carriage trundled along the street, through towering houses, with their white-washed, half-timbered stories—and down and down, past the heights of High Street, and then along River Street, with its heavy stone walls and piers. Where the blocks of stone stood taller than most men. Where the stone descended in a stairway down to the waters with their rushes. On the walls, a handful of maidens, as green and brown as the rushes, perched and made ribbons.

The youngest looked brightly up at the carriage. "Another one! We will—this ball of Queen Shulamith's will do us so much good. So many ribbons and trinkets for it—"

The other women laughed like rippling water. One said, "A ribbon not made never sells, however grand a ball is held."

The youngest looked obediently back to her ribbon, so that Marjorie, looking out the carriage window, saw only bowed heads and neat brown hair. She folded her hands in her lap. The carriage trundled on through a drab and crowded city. It did not look as if it could possibly be a suitable place to bring out a young woman, let alone the only possible one.

The road rose again, though not as much as High Street had risen. Her aunt lived on the river's other bank. Marjorie looked at the masses of buildings where the bank rose, and hoped that the description did not merely indicate which half of the city the house stood in.

She let her breath out. Perhaps the city was more pleasant than it looked, with its narrow streets and endless gray houses. She knew her mother, and her aunt, would never let her leave here again without settling her. If she died an old maid, she would die here. For a minute, her eyes stared out the window without seeing anything. Six months ago, it had all been arranged that she would come with her cousin, and her cousin's husband and their two little boys. Merely because the cousin and husband had died, her mother had thought, was no reason for her not to come out now. She shivered. She had not seen her cousin Artemise in seven years; she had never even met her sons. Perhaps she never would meet the boys, now.

The carriage lurched to a stop and made her blink. Her elderly companion snorted and pulled her black shawl closer.

"Ridiculous, the way people do not—just because the city is rife with exiles, they do not know how to treat gentry— even an exiled king should not be treated like a beggar—a mere entertainer, blocking *our* way!"

Marjorie leaned half out the window. In a square ahead of them, music played—magically, she could see no musicians—and a brown bear danced, hand in paw, with a dark-haired woman in a flame-red gown that flared like a poppy. The woman herself, and the bear, did not stand in the way, but a crowd clumped around—fishwives, peddlers, servants with packages. After all, this was the morning. Even if the gentry, or nobility, or royalty, had risen, they would not be about, to watch. Marjorie let out her breath. Well, except fools like herself, who might be about, for all their higher birth. She did not sit back.

The bear pirouetted, and Marjorie eyed it. She had seen dancing bears before, and poor pitiful things they had been. This bear, with its shaggy brown coat, could *dance*.

The bear's claws, gleaming like ivory, passed very close to the woman, and Marjorie shivered. The woman curtsied the bear bowed, the music ended, and the crowd, with a shower of coins before the dancers, shuddered, and broke up, laughing and chattering. A girl's voice wondered if the bear would come to Queen Shulamith's ball, and Marjorie, sitting back, wondered how long it would take for her to learn that tale.

"Finally!" The companion eyed Marjorie, who looked back at her hands.

The carriage turned a corner. An empty street spread before them.

"At least here they have proper back streets," grumbled the duenna. "Where the riffraff can come to the back door."

The carriage rumbled up before a house looking like many another on this street, and in other streets: square, solid, built of gray stone, four stories with glass windows looking out. Wrought iron, in filigrees more sinuous than vines, stood before the windows.

As her luggage came down, Marjorie stood in the street and tightened her hands on the fabric of her skirt. The day before she would have thought the house tall. Now, after the towering concoctions on High

Street, she could barely keep from thinking them short. But still, she did not like the sight of them.

A window opened. A young woman, still dressed in a morning wrap, her hair a mass of pale brown curls, looked over the ironwork. Marjorie tried to remember who she was, and what her name was, but before she could, the other woman turned back to call, without much enthusiasm, into the house.

"Aunt Maude! She made it! She's here, she's arrived!"

Moments later, the door opened, and Maude, muttering about "this early," swept out with servants to take the luggage. While they hustled it within, she exchanged greetings and farewells with the duenna, and ushered Marjorie inside, to a hall of white-washed walls, with a mirror by the door, ready for a departing woman to give her beauty one last inspection.

The other young woman had come down the stairs. She stood on the last of the dark wood steps and looked vaguely discontented.

"Henrietta," said Maud, "this is Marjorie my niece." She waved at Henrietta. "My goddaughter, come here for the festivities as you have."

Marjorie looked down, at the dark wood of the floor. And for the young men, no doubt.

Maude closed the door and looked her up and down. "Though I dare say her mother readied her better than you. Your hair!"

The journey had not left her hair in wild disarray; she could barely eye it, even out of the corner of her eye. In the mirror, she saw nothing conspicuous about it: pale blond, pretty, perhaps her best feature.

"Whatever did your mother think, letting you dye it? *Quite* out of fashion. Everyone knows that women dye their hair to try to pass themselves off as fairer than they are. Waste of money, she clearly spent a pretty penny to get it that shade. It looks natural."

As if it were not her own, her hand moved up, as stiffly as the arm of a watermill, to pull forward a lock of her hair. It looked as it always had.

"It's blond by nature," said Marjorie, barely audibly.

She had spoken loudly enough to be heard; Maud eyed her and then shrugged.

"We shall just dye it, then. Black, I think. Suits you better than brown. And your eyebrows as well. A good thing we have spells to do the thing properly."

Marjorie stood like stone. And to think her parents had sent her to Maud only because her mother had not wanted to change the timing. Artemise would not have dyed her hair black, even if only because her hair was blond.

Maud bustled her up the stairs. "A pity you will not be ready for King Magnus's fete, but you can't be."

"I can be," said Henrietta. "I've sewed everything. I've spent hours. . .."

"Most improper," said Maude, climbing onward, not glancing at her. "I must get Marjorie ready. If her mother did not have her hair dyed, she must have failed in many things. And you can not go alone."

Henrietta grimaced and still followed them up the stairs, but when Maude bustled Marjorie into a backroom, overlooking the garden, Henrietta continued to walk along the hallway. Marjorie glanced about the room, with its pale yellow wallpaper and the furnishings, and the window overlooking the garden. She got barely a glimpse of the blossoming roses, and the promised back street behind it, before Maude turned on her.

"You do know to hold your tongue about Konigsburg?"

Marjorie nodded. "Konigsburg, and Kingsbury, and any other name. I will speak of the city, and use no other name, which will cause no offense among those from other kingdoms and lands."

"Not just among the fancy," said Maude. "Even the servant and shopkeepers—" She glanced out the doorway and realized her other charge had walked rather slower than she should have. Trying to eavesdrop, no doubt.

"Henrietta, I've told you to avoid pouting like that. You will do it in public and offend people—besides, it is not becoming."

Henrietta grimaced and stalked onward. She had paid attention only long enough to find something to embarrass her. Now, Maude would fuss over Marjorie and pay *her* no more attention than she paid the kitchen cat. No, less—she would curse the cat if it caught no mice. When Marjorie—if she were not silly—would *want* her to go to the fetes and balls. Then she would be introduced, and could introduce Marjorie to all the people when she went. Marjorie would have to like that better than sitting in the corner.

It would even help her be ready for Queen Shulamith's ball.

Henrietta reached her room, where the window overlooked the street, and glowered at the wallpaper. Not that Maude's fussing would prove much help to Marjorie. Already *she* had stayed here three months, and Lady Maude's vaunted sponsorship had not won her so much as a man expressing a wish to know her better. And she had worked so hard to be ready for King Magnus's ball.

She went over to the window. The street did not bustle, but was not utterly empty; a carriage rattled along, like the one that had brought Marjorie. She turned away; it would not be someone calling, not at this hours, and indeed, the carriage rattled on, down the street, about the corner, and up a hillside.

Inside sat two pale-haired little boys, their faces salt white and all the paler by their charcoal gray clothes, their jerkins laced up with dark blue ribbons.

The younger stirred, looked out the window, and said, without much spirit, "Is that the house?"

Michel shook his head, without looking up. Even out of the corner of his eye, he had seen the stone fronting the street. Most of the grown-ups had talked over his head, but he had heard *some* things.

"Not yet, Philippe."

Philippe sank back down, as subdued as Michel. The coach trundled on, turned a corner, and stopped. Michel slowly looked up. A great, pale house stood before them. Between them and it, a wall of white stone held up wrought iron railings, and between that wall and the house, statues stood: a slender young angel, her hands on high, her face imploring; a dragon, every scale distinct, coiled and ready to burn some soul alive; a monkey-like imp posed in some caper; and more. Three gray-barked trees stood among them, their very trunks bent.

The house itself bore more statuary, carved little winged children, and curlicues and festoons about arched windows. It had room enough to hold them both, and half a hundred other children at need; the house stood larger than a king's castle.

"Ho, young masters, we haven't got all day," snarled the coachman, as he climbed down from his seat. "Don't sit like lumps." He hauled open the door, and Michel stumbled out, feeling wobbly, as if the earth lurched the way the carriage had.

"Ho, now," said the coachman. Michel turned. Philippe stood in the carriage's door, blinking. The coachman scooped him down to the ground, none too gently, and said, "To the door, to the door, you think we've got all day?"

"Will the sun set early?" said Philippe, timidly, and the coachman raised his hand, as if to knock him over. Philippe stepped closer to Michel, who took his hand and rushed off with him, toward the house. They hurried along the white flagstones of the path with the coachman stalking after them, through the none-too-green garden, where red mushrooms grew.

Over the steps to the doorway, a snow leopard slumped. Its tufted ears twitched a little in its slumbers, its head rested on its forepaws, and its long sleek body spread as if to annex as much of the stairs as it could. Its pale gray spots flexed as it breathed. Philippe grabbed onto Michel's arm with both hands. Michel tried not to stare. He had to be brave, he couldn't frighten Philippe. . . but they had to live here, in this house, with that creature that slept on the doorstep.

The coachman gawked at it. Then, with a shudder, he reached for the knocker, a fantastic contraption like a knotted ribbon made of lead. It clomped against the door solidly; the noise sounded, but did not echo.

And it did not rouse the snow leopard. It slumbered on, its flanks rising and falling as it breathed.

Clinging to his brother's hand, Michel looked over the garden. Some grass did grow there, though low against the ground. One tree stood bent like the crescent moon, and for a moment, he thought he saw a face in the bark.

The door opened, slowly but silently. From behind it, without moving out of the hall's shadows, an old, old man looked out. He still stood straight, but his white hair foamed about his head and into a beard, and his face bore more wrinkles than a withered old apple. His narrowed eyes looked down at them.

"So these are my great-great-grandsons," he said, his voice scratchy.

The coachman bowed and retreated in silence. Philippe stepped closer to Michel, and Michel's grip tightened.

Their great-great-grandfather sniffed. "The door's open. What fanciness do you need to come in?"

Philippe's hand tightened until he felt like an anchor, but the coach already rattled along the street without them. Michel swallowed. The city had other coaches. Not one would take two orphaned boys with nowhere to go and no coin to pay. He inched inside, and Philippe clung to him, so close that they nearly tripped over each other's feet.

Without so much as stepping back in order to give them a place to stand, their great-great-grandfather peered down at them. His eyes narrowed more—Michel had not realized that was possible—and he sniffed again.

"*What* were they thinking? Your clothing is *far* too merry for children in morning. Such festive ribbons! Blue! When your parents have died!"

Michel looked down at them.

"You will go to the tailor for new clothing." He turned from the door. A desk stood by it, of dark red wood, so tall than even a grown man like their great-great-grandfather had to stand to write at it. His pen scratched, and a minute later, he stamped the letter with red sealing wax, and handed it to Michel. Michel took the letter but stared at it. It could have been a curse that would turn them both into statues, for all he could see. The grotesque gargoyle on the seal grinned back at him.

Philippe pulled closer to him.

"I trust you can recognize a tailor's shop?" said their great-great-grandfather, coldly.

He had seen enough shop signs to know a tailor's. Michel nodded.

"Turn left when you reach the street. Old Wat knows better than to cheat me." He loomed over them. Michel stepped back, out of the doorway again. Philippe stumbled out with him. "The first tailor on the street."

The door shut. The snow leopard yawned, a great gap of scarlet opening in its face. Michel swallowed. It eyed them lazily, as if considering whether two such small mouthfuls were worth the effort of getting up. After a moment, it settled again, its head lazing on its paws, not a hint of red showing.

"Come, Philippe," said Michel, his voice wobbling.

They inched outward, and looked from side to side in the garden, seeing, now, statues like butterflies, and others like snails. But even walking slowly, they reached the street, and Michel walked along it, holding Philippe's hand. As far as he could see down the way, there were no shops at all, not a single sign hanging over the street, or even a building that fronted the street. They plodded on, in front of great houses like their great-great-grandfather's, with their walled gardens, and their pale stone, until his legs ached from the distance.

One house, built of icy white stone, bustled with life as servants arrayed it with flowers, in pots and in garlands, in pinks and reds, and greenery, to conceal the stone. Others put in place statues, to stand on pedestals and walls, and in nooks in the walls, but not statues of the pale stone like their great-great-grandfather's garden. These were metallic and enameled in a glorious array of colors: birds and harlequins, jugglers with their balls, dancers arrayed for a dazzling ball, and many of those with crowns. Phillipe's eyes were round, and he turned his head to watch the servants' work, until he stumbled because he looked behind them. Michel pulled him on, and they looked down the street of pale houses, unadorned.

Behind them, with much profanity and shouted orders, the servants went on with the array, ignoring any passers-by.

"They had best think all this greenery is something fine," grumbled one. "It's worse than statues, with all the prickles."

"As long as they pay for the work, it hardly matters," said another. He shifted the rose garland in his hand, and cursed, looking at the blood a thorn had drawn from his finger, and turned his attention back to the garlands. No time to even notice passers-by. They had to put out the lights as well.

The day inched onward. Servants climbed on ladders to bedeck the niches on the fourth and fifth floors, with blossoms and candles, and the air grew scented with the blooms. At nightfall, with the last leaves and flowers barely in place, flame leapt magically up in lamps and candles, to shine on the guests who swept in. Girls, new to the city, or so young they had not attended such galas before, gawked and had to be hustled onward before they were laughed at as green. Two girls squealed as the older girl pointed out a figure with a red beard and red hair, wearing a golden crown and a suit of metallic peacock green—"Like King Magnus himself!" said the younger.

"Hush," said her mother. "You can not squeal so at a mere party and expect me to take you to Queen Shulamith's ball."

The girl pouted. "You take me to balls, I can go to balls."

"As long as you are well," said her mother. "Girls who can go to balls can still suffer from such *fearful* headaches that they can not go anywhere at all. Queen Shulamith will accept such an excuse and be full of sympathy." She swept up the stairs, her subdued daughters following.

By the doorway, a lean, tall man with gray in his black hair bowed to her. He wore black, that invariable refuge of the poor—feigned mourning to avoid the cost of finer clothing, indifferent to the crowlike air they brought to festivities—and his black was shabbier than most even of them.

He spoke politely enough, bowing and saying, "You were fortunate, my lady. You came just in time for the last dance."

The mother frowned. The ball would last all hours. To end before midnight was a shame, and many lasted until dawn.

"Gemma will leave after this."

She scowled. Such an entertainment, at a ball—and her girls looked delighted.

"The last—" the older one whispered, and they pressed forward, past their mother. The center of the room held a bear. With it stood a woman in a flame-red gown, her black hair floating over her shoulders like a cloak.

Their mother sniffed. "For King Magnus to bring such a creature here, and his keeper is hardly better—we could see this any day on the street."

"And suffer the crowds' impertinence?" said the man.

The music struck up, and her daughters did not stay for the conversation but pressed into the room. The bear held out its paw, the woman took it, and they footed it through a stately measure. The mother muttered that her own daughters should be ashamed, not enraptured, as they did not dance as well as the beast, and others about the hall murmured of the skill as well.

"No common bear, this one," called one young man as Gemma curtsied, and the bear bowed. Gemma's face did not move; it felt like a mask. She still wondered how she did it. It felt strange, as she straightened, not to hear the patter of coins at her feet yet. She knew that their fee would exceed the take on the street, but—how swiftly she had grown accustomed to being a mountebank!

"The bear prince," called a young woman. When every eye turned on her, she blanched and said, more hesitantly, "The—Queen Lenore's third child. She would have taught him to dance, with the rest of a prince's education. . . ." It did not slackening the staring, and her words faltered into silence.

Gemma put her hands on her hips. Her jaw tightened. "The bear prince? Queen Lenore's son? But everyone knows that the bear prince lives with the queen his mother in the forest, in *seclusion*." She waved one hand, sweeping the entire hall and all the guests. "Clearly, then, since he is the bear prince, you are all enchantments that the court magicians conjured to amuse both mother and son. Perhaps you are all really *trees*, and can only move and dance for his delight." She drew the hand back against herself, framing her throat. Mountebank. She had to convince them of that. "Therefore it behooves you all to be generous to us. Your money must be as enchanted and unreal as you yourselves are—stinting will not benefit you—it will dissolve into leaves for you as well as it will for me."

Laughter resounded, and the clink of money on stone. Candlelight glinted from the metal, and Gemma went to gathered up coins with the eagerness they would expect from some poor peasant lass. The bear snuffled at the coins, drawing laughter, and then the crowd eased off, toward some other room, some other amusement, chattering about this ball and that, and whether Queen Shulamith would send them all invitations, and whether the ball could truly match the wonders they saw every month, surely a monarch accustomed to giving balls would do better than one who never did, and whether that would stop anyone from attending.

Gemma did not care, as long as they left; their invitations would not determine hers. As the guests thinned, King Magnus's servants came toward her, picking the coins up. They pocketed at least half of them, she knew, but she eyed them, the bear beside her, and they yielded some.

The bear snorted. Gemma turned. On all fours, its black nose snuffling at the air, the bear leaned toward a whip-lean man, brown in coloring and clothing. Even on all fours, its height came nearly to the man's shoulder. It eyed his hands, and its fangs showed bare and sharp.

"He is *helping* us," scolded Gemma. "Helping gather our coins. You should not be so mistrustful. I am sure he will not steal them." She smiled at the servant. Then she approached and held out her hand. That servant handed over twice as many coins as all his fellows.

Gemma, her mouth twisting, held them out for a moment before pocketing them. "See?"

The bear gave a sound, half snort, half growl, and its paw pushed a coin over the floor. Gemma dropped to one knee to add it to their hoard. Better than the streets, she noted, even without the fee.

Then, thanking the servants but offering not a penny, she went for her cloak, to muffle herself in its dark folds, and she and the bear headed outside and crossed the chessboard of bright and dark where the windows shone down.

King Magnus's house and its light fell behind, and no one else nearby gave a fete on this night; dark, moonless night folded round them. Only a ribbon of stars, directly overhead, was not hidden by the buildings to either side. Gemma shivered. Though the city seemed less oppressive by day than when they had first arrived, she had not gotten used to its night.

"We have no need of the money," said the bear, its voice deep and growling.

"We do," said Gemma, without a glance aside. "We need money enough so that no one will question whether we earned what we spend, or whether we came to the city to earn money."

To that charge, the bear offered no counter-argument. They ambled down the street until Gemma could smell the water of the river as the bear could. There, they headed down a side alleyway to a stable. The horses had all been removed, and the stable cleaned, for the gold Gemma could pay.

She closed the door carefully behind them, shutting them into the dark and the smell of straw, and ensuring no outside light seeped in, before she began her conjuration. It took a minute, with the straw rustling into new shapes, but then they stood in a room with a lit lamp, a heap of rugs to make the bear a bed, and an actual bed for her.

"Easier by daylight." The bear sat on its haunches. "When you don't have to be so careful about the light."

"I'd have timed it closer if I had known that mattered," said Gemma. "It's not as if I brought us back early because I hoped to go to the library."

The bear grunted. Gemma went to the door to look out.

"Don't you?" said the bear. "Hope?"

"Hope, yes," said Gemma. The street outside was empty. "Brought, you may have noticed, no." She stepped into the doorway. "I'm going down to the river, for a breath of air."

She closed the door behind her, quickly. In the cool and the dark, she let her breath out. The bear would go to bed, and she would have to find her way in, in the dark. But she did not think she could have stayed there much longer. He treated her like a servant—

She *was* a servant, Gemma told herself. The night breeze, cooling, tugged at her skirts. Queen Lenore meant well, raising the poor orphan herself, but she should have had her fostered by a suitable family of wizards. She eased her way down the alley. She was not even noble. Yes, her father had been a wizard in Queen Lenore's service, and he had died saving the queen, but a just reward for that was to raise the little orphan and give her her father's place, which Queen Lenore had done. Sending her as a servant with the prince showed how highly the queen trusted her.

When she reached the street, a carriage creaked down it, with four lanterns marking it out. Gemma turned, to walk toward the river. From the clock tower, the clock face gleamed like a moon, but Gemma did not even glance at it, as the hour hardly mattered. The air smelled of water and rushes. Light glowed among the rushes, and Gemma's mouth twisted. The women there no doubt conjured homes out of mud, as she did from straw, and wove their ribbons from flowers. Or rushes, and then used magical dyes.

Under the bridge itself, fires burned, surrounded by the other entertainers of the street. They wore a mix and match of the brilliance of their costumes and drab, sensible travel wear. The fire gilded parts of the scene and cast enormous shadows over the rest.

A boy plucked at a lute, a tune drifting over the waters. A dark young woman—Gemma had seen her dancing, and hailed as "the elegant Esmeralda"—shook out her green skirt, and her gaze fell across Gemma.

"Ho, fellows," Esmeralda called, her voice ringing. "Watch what secrets we tell." She shook the skirt harder. "We have a *rival* watching us."

Gemma stopped. All the eyes had turned on her, firelight glinting from eyeballs and casting shadows over their faces. After a minute, when none of them turned away, she said, thinly, "You have new dances for my bear?"

Laughter echoed raucously from stone and waters. Gemma drew back, along the bank. The city's enchantments made its streets safer than most, but she did not quite turn her back on them until the firelight vanished behind her, and there was the clock's light—as bright as a half moon, at least.

Another light gleamed across the river: bobbing along. A candle-man, thought Gemma. A plump man wrapped in ramshackle coats of bright reds and purples, with his candles arrayed about the brim of his hat—he ambled along with their usual leisure. Two little charges, fair-haired and dressed in black, scurried alongside, or fell back and hurried to join up again, because slow though his pace was, he did not slow further when the boys were not by him. She scowled, but—what could she do? Being scolded by a woman who danced on the street with a bear would hardly frighten a candleman, especially without the bear.

He proceeded down the street, out of her sight, and the boys ran after. A moon-pale owl flitted, silently, after them. In the moments when it caught such light as there was, no one saw it, and moments later it veered off into an alleyway. The candleman trudged on.

Philippe, catching up, looked warily up at him. Michel kept his gaze to the street, but the candleman, with his bleary eyes and blood-shot face, frightened Philippe. Even that great, broad-brimmed hat with a row of candles around the edge: they shed light, but he did not like it.

"What's that?" said Michel, pointing to the light across the river. Philippe peered, following his finger to under the bridge: a reddish glow, like a fire.

"Eh," said the candleman, without looking aside, "who knows? No-body who matters, down by the river. Even by day, only time the fancy go down is to buy ribbons." He turned, and they crossed a bridge to the other side, and up the street. Michel yawned, and felt no more curiosity about the light. He peered ahead hoping for his great-great-grandfather's house before he fell asleep in the street.

Something—something small—floated through the air ahead.

The candleman said, sullenly, "Eh, do not like this Winter Street. Tailor shoulda paid more. I'd've made him, knew it was Winter Street."

Michel scowled at the little flecks. Were they really—then he put out his tongue and caught one snowflake on it. It melted. He looked at Philippe, who looked back with enormous eyes.

But as they walked on, the boys stumbling from exhaustion, snow sifted over the street, and the stones grew slick. Philippe slipped on one rounded one, and Michel ran to help him. His legs hurt, they had walked for so long, and stood for so long to be fitted.

"Come along, boys, come along," said the candleman, not breaking his stride, his voice containing no encouragement. "In the snow, it's not wise to linger on the street."

Michel glared at him, and the boys scrambled to keep up, stifling their yawns.

Their great-great-grandfather's house finally stood ahead. The candlelight shot enormous shadows up against the walls and in the hollows of the sculptures, distorting the statuary into unrecognizable forms, with mouths and claws that seemed ready to snatch.

Michel and Philippe clung to each other's hands, peering about, as they walked toward the door, and Michel tripped over the candleman's heels. He did not even glance back. Michel peered around him to see the snow leopard still asleep on the doorway. Snow had drifted up beside it.

"Ho, now, I delivered you home, that was my instruction, and so I bid you good day." The candleman walked off, more briskly than he had walked with them. The candle flames swirled with his passage, sending the shadows whirling, shrinking, swelling, and Michel scrambled past the leopard to knock on the door.

The knocker was loud, left no echo, and stirred no response. For all Michel could tell, as the sound faded, the house had long been abandoned and hollow, with no one having set foot in it for many a day, or year. Even the leopard was not roused. He bit his lip and tried the door. It opened, still silently. Though the air was warmer, the light was even less inside than out. Splotches of moonlight, through the windows, lay along the hallway like the pale spots of a dark leopard.

The leopard yawned and shifted.

The boys scrambled inside, and Michel shut the door as swiftly as it would move. It closed with a clunk heavier than the knocker's, stirring neither echo nor any movement.

They stood for a minute. The air was still, and a trifle warmer than outside. Moonlight filtered through enormous windows, showing long whitewashed halls, with winding staircases built of dark wood, and doors of the same wood.

Michel let his breath out. "Let's go to bed," he said, trying to sound brave, and the words echoed a little.

"How?" said Philippe. "*He* didn't say where to sleep. Didn't—" He yawned. "—see anywhere instead."

"Some rooms here have to have beds," said Michel.

Philippe eyed the stairs. "What if—" His voice grew smaller, more ghost-like. "What if we find *his* bedroom?"

Michel swallowed. "Then we'll ask him where to sleep," he said, though his voice trembled.

They climbed to the next floor, with moonlight falling on their steps now and again. There, they tried door after door, each of which opened silently on rooms lined with books, or set with tables and chairs, or even nothing at all, only a bare four walls and windows. If they had found only one with a couch, he would have dared it, but they did not.

They did not speak loudly, but their voices echoed despite themselves, and when they had passed, the dark wood seemed darker, and the pale walls paler. Finally, they found a small, whitewashed room with a lead-paned window and two small beds. A servant's room, thought Michel, but there, they crawled in, to sleep within moments. The house lowered with disapproval about them. Even the owls, bats, and pale moths gave it a wide berth by moonlight, and none of the morning's birdsong came from its trees.

The house still lowered on, even as the next day grew bright and cloudless. The passersby, afoot or in carriage, tended to hurry by it. When Maude's carriage trundled by, Marjorie eyed it. Even among the great mansions. . . .

"That's an unpleasant place," she said.

Maude shrugged. Marjorie turned to face her. Her own hair shifted in the movement, and she winced. She wondered when the sight would no longer startle her, those raven tresses instead of her own honey blond, but Maude had set to at once, to leave nothing to chance.

"It's not like the old man living there cares much," said Henrietta, oblivious to her thoughts, not even looking out the window. "I mean, his *great-grandson* just died. Old man, probably thinking of his grave and not his house."

The carriage trundled on, and Marjorie, doubting she would get any other answer, sighed and sat back. If the old man gave balls or even teas, Henrietta would, no doubt, manage interest, for all his age—and Maude would be the same. She tilted her head back. And she would, too, she had to admit. Her parents would never free her from Maude's—tutelage until she married. However many years that took. And she would spend all of them with her hair dyed black.

For a moment, she frowned, remembering something about her dead cousin, her husband, and his great-grandfather. But it did not come clearly to her.

"Look," said Henrietta, "beggars." She pointed out a crossroads ahead, at drab, ragged figures there. "They're always there. We shall have to be careful." She turned a triumphant smile on Marjorie.

"Of course we shall," said Maude, sedately.

Marjorie looked at her hands, not willing to look up at Henrietta's smirk.

"We know this is a danger," said Henrietta, leading forward. "Taking you to the riverside. But we will watch you. In case some child falls in—"

"And *watch*," said Marjorie, "is *all* you will do. You won't stop me. And I will come back to drip all over you and all over the carriage, and all your newly purchased finery." She leaned forward. "And get you so wet you will sicken for the rest of the season."

Henrietta gaped as if she had forgotten how to close her mouth. Lady Maude watched Marjorie, and Marjorie had to fight to keep from looking away, like a child who had just stolen jam.

The carriage trundled to a halt, jolting her from her thoughts. By the riverside, a building rose not from the bank but from the river, and the very wood of it seemed green. Maude and Henrietta set out briskly from the carriage, and Marjorie, having no wish to look a country chit, hurried with them.

Inside, great racks held every color of clothing, every ribbon, in lace or a band, every kind of button and notion, with customers scuttling among them. Slim, willowy woman, supple and as brown as river water, flourished their fares so that the air seemed filled with them, like a cascade of flowers at a May festival, and all the fancy ladies nodded gravely and discussed merits of this shade or that. Marjorie managed to walk several steps from the door, but no farther, before she stopped to gawk like a country chit.

"My lady!" One woman came up to her. Her skin had more than a touch of green to it, and her dark eyes glanced over Marjorie and glinted like a river wave in the sun. "You will need gowns for your season here." Maude and Henrietta came up behind her—Henrietta looking as if she had bitten something sour—and Marjorie nodded.

"You have come to the right place." She smiled. "All honest mirrors here—not so magical as Lady Shulamith's—because we have only to show you the truth!"

Cloth and ribbon floated about her, Maude insisting on this, or scornfully dismissing that, without letting Marjorie speak so much as a word, until Maude proclaimed it done and paid out

the coins. A thin little girl scooped up the cloth to lug it out to the carriage. Maude had purchased some things for Henrietta, but the bulk of it—Marjorie stared at the heap—was hers.

The girl flumped the package down in the carriage and grinned, gap-toothed, at Marjorie. "You'll have a dress like springtime."

"So you will," said Maude, ushering her charges inside the carriage. "Tonight, for Lady Celestine's. One night's waiting was enough. If we sew with enough speed, we will have a gown ready for you." Her mouth twisted. "And you will have proof of your sewing skill, if a bridegroom, or his mother, insists on that."

Henrietta pouted. Maude turned on her.

"And, yes, you must sew on it as well. Sew your own tomorrow. It will not even help you by contrast. If they see that your godmother can not fitly prepare her niece, it will reflect poorly on *you*."

Without another word, Maude leaned back against the seat and closed her eyes. Henrietta looked banefully at Marjorie as the carriage trundled along the street, stopping, turning, and climbing hills. A flight of sparrows twittered, swirling about the carriage, and then upward towards the sun. A girl at Queen Hesione's school looked out the window toward them, and leaned forward to see the street and the carriage, and sighed.

"They went to get cloth for ball gowns," she pronounced. "They will go to Queen Shulamith's ball in them."

Her gaze came back to the room. It moved over the book before her, without taking in the words, to settle on her own sleeve, the drab brown of the upper girls' uniform.

"She won't hold a ball when we can go," she pronounced.

"Like we should, Lucy," said Carol, sternly. "No one knows much about Queen Shulamith—not even what kingdom she came from—and look at the wild stories about her mirrors—how can they even know she's a queen, really?"

"Well, it's rude to pry," said Lucy.

"So many exiles," chimed in young Mariana. "And all their sad stories. It's so very rude to question a royal lady and recall all her woes to her."

All the girls bobbed their heads—how tragic that would be, to cause such sorrow to such a highborn and elegant queen—and Carol muttered, under her breath, "A *rich* royal lady."

"She looks like a queen," said Mariana. "All regal and stately, and—queenly."

Carol laughed, shortly. "Like an actress playing a queen. You'd think Queen Tatiana wasn't a queen, all short and squat and with her ugly face all set in mean lines and dressing up in lace and fur so she looks like a pillow—but she's a queen. Only in penny dreadfuls is a queen in exile always young and lovely and sad."

"But—"said Nina, slowly and dreamily emerging from her book, "don't you know, usually? You don't have to ask them. Their servants talk to the butcher, the flower girl, the milkman—bits and pieces, it all comes out."

Lucy nodded. "We heard that Queen Jane's kingdom was offering her the crown back—with a constitution, but still a crown—'cause only a monarch would let them to enter *here*, the City, with ambassadors and everything." She tilted her head to one side. "Her servants talked to *everyone*."

"*Hers* don't," said Carol, portentously. "Queen Shulamith's servants hold their tongues as if Queen Shulamith had them witched—and who ever heard of a queen who was a witch, too?"

"A student who read her history, young Carol," said Queen Hesione, crisply, from the doorway. "If you have so much time to gab, perhaps we should move more briskly. I do not wish your parents to complain that you are not learning so swiftly as you could, when you have so much to learn."

She walked into the room, turning her gaze on Carol. "With what you have said, I must begin at the beginning—do you even know how the city came to be? Who was so silly as to build a city for those who fled their native lands?"

Carol's tongue felt like lead in her mouth. "It wasn't," she stammered. "For exiles. It was for kings. It was magic—they could all come to it with a day's journey, and they did to make peace. So—" She drew a deep breath, and the words came more clearly. "They came again and again. When they had make treaties. Or when they wanted to show off their sons and daughters, for marriages. It was only when there were wars driving them off that they came here as exiles. And when there were *revolutions*, they came. Lots and lots and lots."

Queen Hesione looked a little pale, as if she had not realized this would remind her of her own midnight escape to here, but her voice was cold and clear.

"And so—how do we know that Queen Shulamith is a queen indeed?"

Carol's mouth opened and shut. Finally, she said, weakly, "Because she's here?"

Queen Hesione raised an eyebrow.

"She wouldn't be able to find her way here without royal blood," said Carol, slowly. "They didn't want impostors, or assassins." She started to ponder how the city and its enchantments had managed when kingdoms had changed dynasties.

"Unless she came in an entourage," said Lucy, brightly. "Not everyone here's a king or queen." She spread her hands, having just enough tact not to mention the students did not all have royal blood. "A whole city full of people working—they couldn't all be kings or queens."

Swallows twittered outside, perching on the carvings of ribbons and bows. As the girls recited on, the swallows took wing, flying up and about, and swirling about the houses where seamstresses and daughters bent over fine gowns, and mothers standing over them, urging that now of all times, they had to be proper for every ball—else, they might not be invited to Queen Shulamith's ball.

At the little taverns at the corners, messengers chortled over how much gold was to be found, with all the letters flying about, making plans for the ball.

"Just wait until Queen Shulamith sends her invitations," said one messenger. "She'll hire messengers right and left."

"Huh," said an old man, perched by the fire place that held only ashes. "They don't send 'em like that unless they've got no messengers of their own."

"She doesn't," the messenger assured him. "When have you heard of any message from her establishment?"

"When have you heard anything of her servants?" said the tavern-keeper's daughter, as she filled another mug. "She has them—but nothing's been heard of them."

"Not even," said one man, looking up from his cup, "rumors. You'd think someone'd claim to have been told by a friend of a friend of something someone said."

The messenger fell silent with the rest. A flight of sparrows twittered by the store, and rising and sinking, they flew down the streets, until they flew around the preparations at Lady Celestine's, and the upper room where Lady Celestine listened as her daughter Giselle complained.

"They all care only about Queen Shulamith's ball, as if they even knew anything about what sort of balls she would give—as if there aren't twenty balls a month—as if it might not be the most tedious thing that the city could offer." Giselle wrung her hands. "And I want. . .."

"No man will want to marry you," said Lady Celestine coldly, "if you stand about and whine. Go and see to the decorations." She swept off.

Giselle watched her go and, feeling flat, descended the stairs. One worker draping a red rose garland over the arched doorway noticed her and groaned, jabbing his elbow toward the woman for the benefit of the others. They bent their attention back to the garland, intent as if they had never seen the daughter of the house, hoping she would only pass by them instead of giving more orders.

She floated by.

Other workers, with other garlands, went grumbling out to hang more on the walls. And more. And still more as sparrows twittered about them. The mass of the garlands was so great that the workers barely had time to scramble down the ladders and bear them away as the first carriages trundled up. Followed by many more. The stream of them spread out so far that Marjorie could see them from the window.

"Come along," said Lady Maude, without glancing at her, and Marjorie gathered her skirts and followed.

The gown itself, which they had gotten done in time, was pleasant enough, rosy and green, but Marjorie did not look forward to the fittings for the other fabrics, even while they walked to the carriage as the first stars came out in the violet velvet of the sky, and it bore them down the streets to Lady Celestine's.

Lady Celestine herself, her hair silvery-white and her gown blue with silver threads woven through it, came to greet them and exclaim over how striking Maude's charges were before she led them into a room glowing with candles. It reminded Marjorie of many a party she had attended even before they sent her here. The thought did not calm her.

She took the filigree chair Lady Celestine offered here, a chair so delicate and intricate that she did not dare sit back. Perched there, she chatted with the others, telling them about her journey here and eating the dainty comfits that Lady Celestine's servants brought about.

More people glanced across the room and talked about her—Lady Marjorie, Lady Maude's niece, sent here by her parents—some disgrace? or did she live in some countrified corner?

"Not," said one lady, over her cup, "that she could perhaps find a better bridegroom here. Young gentlemen want gracious and prudent wives, ones who will not disgrace them by their lumpish country ways."

Her companion smirked. "And she dyed her hair, no doubt. Such childishness."

"Hardly," said the first, with more gravity. "Only a fool would dye her hair *such* a shade. Blond, the boys like the fair-haired ones."

A snort answered her, and a voice that carried clearly. "The *boys*, yes. Any prudent woman will take care to avoid such boys."

Silvio, new come to the party, eased past the gossips to see the woman they talked of. Easy enough to pick her out: every other woman in the room had long lived in the city, and attended half a dozen balls that he had had to squire them at.

"The new woman—rather pretty," he said to his cousin.

Luc eyed Marjorie for longer, and Silvio's mouth twitched.

"Rather pretty," Luc agreed. "Though it's odd to see such pale eyes with such—dark hair."

Silvio smirked. And then he heard a squeal behind him.

"Silvio!" His young cousin Nina threw her arms about him, and he kissed and greeted her and wondered aloud that her mother had let so young a girl attend parties. Then, the posy of bright-eyed girls, about the same age, flooded about the two of them with exclamations of how glad they were to see them.

"Though," said one, "we *wonder*." Her mouth pursed. "We see you so seldom, we wonder what you are about in the city."

Silvio threw his hand in the air. The lace fell back from his wrist. "To be sure, we have things to do besides gawk at the ladies—even in this city, we are still young cavaliers."

"Though," said Luc, dryly, "we do not get into as many fights as we might, back home."

"An insult!" said Silvio. "Sir, I demand satisfaction!"

Luc looked at his side, where no sword hung, and his mouth twisted. The girls laughed, their hands going up to their faces, but behind them, older guests scowled.

Celestine's cousin Aurore came through the crowd. Her delicate little face was set in firm lines.

"Now that you have amused us all for a moment, you must come and meet my cousin Marjorie. New arrived in the city—and you would rather gad about with conjured swords, or hunt something up in a storeroom! Making her think we are all ready to take to the streets in a troupe as soon as our king is deposed!"

Silvio smiled but followed as well. Luc said, "Is she Celestine's cousin as well?"

"No," said Aurore. "A second cousin, on my mother's side." She bustled them through the crowd, which subsided back to their gossip (however much the two of them would feature in it), and Marjorie politely rose to greet them. Silvio flourished his bow as elegantly as he would have danced—or fought a duel.

Luc thought he could hardly match Silvio's verve—but at least he could assure his father that he had made an effort to meet marriageable ladies, even if he had not won a post with a king. There being no point in wasting his trip here, even if it was the done thing for a young man.

Luc bowed over her hand and straightened. After a moment, she raised an eyebrow.

He nearly blushed. He had not moved at all—"I beg your pardon, my lady, I was noting your eyes. Such an uncommon shade of hazel: almost golden."

Marjorie laughed, shortly. Her companion pursed her mouth, her sour expression not faltering beneath her masses of curls. Luc nodded to her. Henrietta, he recalled.

"Her lovely eyes," Henrietta murmured. "How familiar."

"It is as old as ladies' lovely eyes," said Luc, and Marjorie laughed again, more naturally.

Aurore smiled. "My cousin sent for that woman, Gemma, to entertain us. She should arrive at any moment—you will see that you have nothing like it outside the city."

Marjorie's smile seemed a little wry. Moments later, a bustle by the backdoor declared the arrival, and people drifted toward the room.

"Will there be dancing after?" said Henrietta.

"Only if this—Gemma and her bear do not overawe us all," said Aurore, "and make us fear to emulate them."

Luc snorted. A dancing bear overawing them—he knew how the exiles of society took to fancies. He offered Marjorie his arm. Silvio blinked, and then offered Aurore his. Henrietta pouted and trailed behind as they walked over, and into the candlelit room.

"It is worth seeing," said Marjorie, meditatively. "I have seen her dancing on the streets—and at other balls."

Luc raised an eyebrow.

"Every ball I've attended at the city, in fact."

He forced a chuckle. "A popular sight, then, I must see the spectacle before I seem a bumpkin, not having witnessed—" And then they were in the room itself, and he fell silent.

The bear's brown fur gleamed by the candlelight. The woman beside him flamed in her red gown. Her pale face gleamed beside her black hair as she looked about the room. Her gaze settled on the musicians.

They stirred themselves to play, a delicate little tune. Gemma turned to the bear, which rose on its hind legs and bowed deeply to her. She curtsied as deeply in return.

Luc's eyebrows went up. "That's more than you expect from a dancing bear," he whispered to Silvio. Silvio grunted, not looking away. Luc stepped back to whisper the same to Marjorie. Slowly, she nodded.

Hand just touching paw, bear and woman moved through the measures of the intricate dance. The crowd about them thickened with more and more of those attending, but neither dancer let that perturb their steps.

When the dance ended, the woman curtsied, the bear bowed, and the watchers applauded with enthusiasm.

From the crowd came Lady Celestine's cool, amused voice. "Since it so pleases you, let us have another." Again Gemma curtsied, and the bear bowed. Lady Celestine nodded to the musicians, who struck up a merrier tune, and Gemma and the bear danced again, with nimble steps as they twirled about each other.

"She had best not let it go on too long," said Marjorie to Luc, softly. "We will be overawed and unwilling to dance ourselves for fear of contrast. There must be dancers here who would fear to fall below the bear's skill."

Silvio's mouth twitched as Gemma swirled about, her skirt flaring. Many a dancer in the city would be wise to find the contrast disheartening. But the clumsiest ones, and the heaviest on foot, would continue to dance on everyone else's toes; if they could be discouraged, they would have been.

Lady Celestine called for a third dance, and Gemma and the bear moved through a stately one, but after it, Lady Celestine spoke of their all taking to the dance floor. Gemma collected her coins and angled off with the bear, toward some back door. Silvio heard Luc asking Marjorie to dance, behind him. Many a woman, standing there, could dance with him, but Silvio angled off himself. Behind the dancing room, two pale stairs lead down to the doorway; they curved around into shadow, but the dancing music still reached down there. Gemma walked down one stair, and Silvio, hurrying a little, darted down the other to reach the landing before her.

Gemma started and climbed back up a stair. The bear growled, and its ivory teeth were large and sharp.

Silvio bowed, deeply. "Forgive me, my lady. But be assured I mean no harm." He smiled, though it felt forced even to him. "Your—chaperon surely would keep you safe from any harm."

Gemma snorted, eyeing him.

"Such an admirable dancer. Listen: the dance begins." He held out a hand. "If you humor an impudent rascal, you make escape with nothing more than a trodden on toe, if he proves a worse dancer than your usual companion."

The bear growled. Gemma eyed the door. Still, she held out her hand. Silvio, grinning, took it, and led her into the graceful measures. The bear lurked on the stairs, watching them move in and out of shadow. Gemma even smiled after a minute: impudence was all she could fault in him; he danced more elegantly than many a dancer master she had had.

The music ended. For a moment, Silvio stood there, holding her hand. Then he freed it and bowed. "I shall return to the rest of the dancers, my lady—spoiled for them—you dance as exquisitely as—one would think you learned at court."

Gemma wondered how she managed a smile, but she felt her face move, however stiffly. Though she doubted she could betray more. If he knew—if he even guessed—that she had come from a court, she could only hope that his honor would make him hold his tongue.

He went up the stairs to where the next tune began, back into the candlelight.

Gemma drew in a deep breath. Voices slipped down the stairs.

"Oh so fancy," said one, full of venom. "Like she knows nothing but entertaining the high-born. But you'll see her dancing on the streets come morning for any beggar's brat. Gold, gold, gold—she thinks nothing but of gold!"

A deep, full laugh followed. "And you begrudge her? She will need every coin she can get. She entertains every ball. She is in fashion. Once she is out—I hope she's wise enough to save, she'll be out one day soon."

Her breath gushed out. Coin was one thing, but—she went down to the door, her heart hammering, and the bear on her heels—if she went out of fashion before Queen Shulamith's ball, both the balls and the streets were in vain. She would need to find some other way in. Her mouth tightened. Perhaps the threat of being mauled by a bear, if it came to that.

The door opened, they hurried outside, the door closed behind them, and as it shut out even the little light of the stairway, the bear growled, "What was he up to?"

For a moment, she blinked. He? The money—and her thoughts fell into place.

Her heart still hammering, Gemma turned from the door. He must be worried, to speak so close to the place. "Mischief," she croaked. "The city is full of them. Young men, exiles, or escapees from their father's houses, with no duties." She let out her breath. "Some of them have money enough for it."

The bear's voice deepened. "And no honor, to plague you so. When you could not face him at law."

"He could have done much, much worse," said Gemma. She hurried from the building, to where light spattered on the pavement from the windows, and looked back up. "See, there he is." She gestured up. The light by the window let her see inside, where Silvio laughed with an old woman. The bear eyed him dubiously, but the young man did not even notice him, lost in the shadows below, when he had his social duties to perform. At least the mirth of dancing with Gemma would make the rest less tedious.

Lady Dagmar patted him on the hand. "I know you, young Silvio. You are here to see how many hearts you can break."

"You know me too well, Lady Dagmar," said Silvio. "Though I do not feel guilty enough to become a hermit yet, perhaps I should leave, surrender my share of these festivities, to mortify my mean-spirited desire."

Dagmar chortled. "And you do not know me at all if you think I can not see when you have grown weary of a party!"

Silvio smiled, but his gaze went about the room. Luc stood opposite, with all the dancers between them. He did not look to break hearts, let alone escape the city by marrying well; he did not talk to, let alone flirt with, the woman by him. Then Silvio marked how his gaze followed Marjorie as she moved through the measures. His eyebrows went up. Luc flirted very badly, and had never been one to fall in love every springtide. He nodded to Lady Dagmar and eased his way about the party. He took up a glass of wine, to ease his throat and disguise his purpose, but only exchanged greetings and walked on. Luc, no doubt, would work out whether he wished to marry her without squiring Marjorie to every dance.

Luc looked over as he approached.

"We should leave before we wear out our welcome, perhaps," said Silvio.

Luc looked back at Marjorie—but here, two dances with the same lady would never be permitted. Silvio's mouth twisted. Luc looked like he would chafe at only three, at a ball, but he shook his head and looked away, determined.

"Let us go," he said. After a moment, he smiled. "Is there any reason to go by the streets?"

Silvio considered and glanced about. If they went into that room—"No, there isn't." He drained his glass and put it aside.

Luc led the way through the crowd, smiling and exchanging greetings, but not stopping. He caught Marjorie's gaze to bow his farewell; Silvio, smiling wryly, also bowed, and Marjorie inclined her head. She shouldn't have dyed her hair that color, he thought, it did not become her. Dismissing her from his thoughts, he followed Luc out of the great hall and the candlelight.

The side doorway led them into a room lit only by the stray candlelight from the party. Windows, as tall as a man, arched up, showing the building outside—another house, without its windows so lit—and a sky of a deep purple. Luc picked one window and opened it. A cart rumbled by, far below, but he looked at the roof, overhead.

"Best one?" said Silvio.

Luc nodded, and reached up. If they had not been on the highest floor already, they would have had to find their way to the attic, but here, Luc's fingers bit the eaves, and he swung himself up. Silvio came closer—this was always the tricky part—but with Luc on the roof, he scrambled up to join him.

The house had shielded the sunset, which still gleamed in the west—but only the darkest shades of red and indigo. The gabled buildings were dark against it.

On the roof itself, Silvio moved with more ease. Light-footed, he climbed up to the gable.

"The view isn't that much better up here," said Luc, "and if we are leaving, we should leave." He ran along the rooftop and leapt to the next house. Silvio, laughing, ran after.

The houses on this street were simple enough—of a height, and without large gardens at their sides. But the street ahead was wider than many. Luc ran the faster, and leapt, and the great, easy arc bore him up and over. Silvio thought he heard a squeak from the street below before he hurtled himself over the gap. He laughed. A newcomer to the city, who did not know why people carefully locked their upper story windows in this city, or that a man walking with care was in more danger than one running.

They could prevent anyone without royal or noble blood from using their escape routes, but for those who had it, the paths were easy enough.

Luc had already leapt off, heading along High Street. The straightest route back to his rooms. Silvio's eyebrows went up, and he chased after.

"Eager to be home?" he said, dryly.

Luc glanced sideways at him. "If you don't think you're up to it—"
He ran again. Silvio chased him as up the streets. At one corner, a
solemn young man glowed as he strummed his lute, and sang below a
single lit window, without a shadow showing at it. He must have enchanted himself for this serenade.

They leapt from his beloved's home to the next building, and he
gawked, the lute producing a tangle of notes. Silvio laughed, on the other side. "That's no way to win a love, fumbling like that."

Luc smiled. "No telling. Have you never seen a woman cooing over
the man who lost on a fight on her behalf?"

Silvio snorted and ran on. Luc chased him, and they bounded up
to the library.

There, great glass windows filled the skylights, showing the round
tower, the shelves of books on every floor, the pale birds that flew across
the open air. Silvio and Luc leapt the glass as well, giving no more heed
to their flight than the birds did to them, though one had flown to
the books at the very height, right under their path. She wrestled out
a book with her beak, took it in her claws, and began the slow circle
down, through air smelling faintly of paper.

She reached the floor; still in the air, she transformed. A pale
woman in pale robes held the book. A thin figure, swathed in a black
cloak, his head covered with a dark hood that shadowed his face,
stepped eagerly forward. The librarian bowed her head and gave the
book into his hands. He scuttled off. She stood there, shaking her head.

"Really," murmured another librarian by her ear, "those spies never
even think to put those impossible cloaks in brilliant colors. You don't
even have to wait until they ask for one of those books."

"I've seen them in green," she said. "Or blue."

"But dark of either shade, which is not much help." The other librarian shook her head. "I'm afraid that the news will be all over the city
at dawn."

The librarian snorted. "It will never take that long."

As the spy scuttled down the steps, the servants out on midnight errands, and the craftsmen at work in their shops for orders that had to be delivered the next day, looked up long enough to see him, and the excited whispers began. A spy—it was likely that there would be an invasion, and all the streets echoed with the news.

One baker cuffed his apprentices back to work with the comment that they should wonder over Queen Shulamith's ball instead. "She's never had a ball before, but even the youngest of you have seen an invasion."

"But we're not baking for Queen Shulamith's ball," said the youngest apprentice, with flour over him like the dirt of the wooer secretly living as a gardener before he fights for the princess's hand in the tourney.

The baker clouted him, sending the flour flying. "Just because you're the youngest of three princes, you still work here *baking bread*, not *talking nonsense*." He harrumphed and turned away, and the rumors rippled around the bakery. A tailor's apprentices walked by, having to refuse to buy pastries before they delivered the clothes they had finished, and walked on, wondering who the invaders were, and whether anyone in the city knew them.

"They don't always invade on the excuse that someone's taken refuge here," said the younger.

The older apprentice shook his head. "They don't need to."

"Well, yes." The younger one hitched up the black clothing in his arms. "They just say that the city lies within their realm and was seized— " He tried to wave his hand in the air and desperately clutched the clothing. "Like there's anyone in the city who controlled it *now*."

The older shook his head. They turned a corner. "They don't have to *realize* they know someone in the city. There's too many people here. I don't think there's any lands where *someone* hasn't run away to come here." The gates of the house appeared ahead of them. "It's not called the city of exiles for nothing. . . ."

They both stared at those pale steps, with the snow leopard slumbering on them. The older apprentice did not wonder that the master had sent them and not come himself.

The curtains on a window twitched. Though neither prentice looked up, they were clearly seen on the street.

"It's the tailor's 'prentices," said Michel. "With our new clothes."

Philippe, slumped against the hearth, shook his head. "Don't want to."

Michel stepped closer.

Philippe looked up and pouted. "Great-great-grandpa never sees us. Never sees what we wear."

"He'll see *them*," said Michel gloomily. He left the room and went down the long corridor. His footsteps echoed, faintly. After a minute, he heard Philippe's, behind him; he started down the winding stairway, and Philippe's feet pattered as he ran to catch up.

He opened the door to the outside. The apprentices looked up. They gawked at him, and then glanced behind him. When only Philippe appeared there, the older one swallowed and said, "We've got the clothes."

Michel held the door open wide. The apprentices eyed the snow leopard and edged up the stairs, keeping as wide a berth as they could. Across the street, six golden horses, drawing a golden carriage, pranced up to the house. A company of soldiers in green and gold surrounded it.

"Which way do the wardrobes lie?" said the older apprentice sharply. Michel looked up at him; his face was vague, and the apprentice felt a pang. The boys looked less lively than when they had arrived at the tailor's. Perhaps they felt their parents' death more.

That wasn't his fault, and there weren't even any servants here to take charge of the clothing. Would serve the lord right if they laid them down in the hallway. But when Michel led them off, the apprentices followed.

And perhaps news would enliven them. "Have you heard of the invasion?" he asked as they climbed the stairs.

"Invasion?" said Michel, stupidly.

"Cross the street?" said Philippe. When the older apprentice looked at him, astounded at so silly a question, Philippe added, "Soldiers."

Both the prentices laughed, though the sound was strangely muffled, dying off without resounding through the corridors. Neither one quite liked the noise.

The younger prentice said, quickly, "No one would be fool enough to try to conquer the city with that few soldiers."

"Though only a fool would try with any number," said the older one, with relish. When the boys looked back in incomprehension, he looked about. "Where are the wardrobes?"

Michel led on. The prentices followed them down the corridor, hung the clothing in the wardrobe, said that it was just as well that neither of them were old enough to go to Queen Shulamith's ball, with only mourning to wear, and went out to find those who could talk of the invasion.

Michel followed them down to close the door and looked across the street. Both the horses and the carriage had vanished, leaving only the drab front of the house.

"Play in the garden?" said Philippe.

After a moment, Michel nodded. They wouldn't even have to change. Even Great-Great-Grandfather couldn't complain if they didn't wear mourning when they weren't going about the city.

"In the back garden," he said.

They wandered down back stairs, narrow and steep, not meant for lordly types, and reached the marble of the garden, under a sky covered with dove-gray clouds. Some plants grew scattered about the stones: rosebushes as tangled as the trees, with a few pale blooms, and more dark thorns than they had leaves. Philippe stared up at one glowering statue of a hairy man with a bull's head but went on when Michel tugged on his hand, and they came to broad stairs, leading down to a pool. A pool that held goldfish, some as small as Philippe's thumb, some as long and thick as Michel's forearm, all of them as pale as ghosts—some tinged with gold, others with spots of flaming orange, still others with nothing at all, only bone-white scales.

"Ghosts of goldfish," said Michel, "they're still gold."

Philippe scowled, and Michel half-agreed. A gold like cream, almost white—"We should get bread from the kitchen, and feed them the crumbs."

Philippe looked up, almost bright-eyed.

"We could lure them up from the depths."

"Oooo!" said Philippe, and Michel smiled back at him. They could see if all the fish were as pale as those they could see.

"Could you now?"

The woman's voice was cold and—dusty, though Michel. Philippe looked at him with enormous eyes, and they both turned toward the stairs.

A woman stood at the top of the stairs. Her face and hair and clothing all were pale brown that was almost gray in drabness, and she was so round that Michel thought of river rocks, piled on each other.

She looked from one to the other of them with her pale eyes. "Shush, both of you," she said. "And no mischief about bread." She went down a couple of the stairs, and then fluttered her hands at them. "Be off with you."

Philippe grabbed Michel's hand. Michel led him off, up the stairs opposite the woman. He could almost feel the woman's eyes on his back as they climbed, but he did not want to look back and slow himself.

"She *scares* me," whispered Philippe.

"She's scary," whispered Michel. "But we won't feed the fish, and she won't. . . ."

Philippe's nose twitched. "She's so fat, she wants to eat all the bread *herself.*"

Michel giggled, and they ran up the last steps. More statues stood about, several of them looking balefully down, but one slender woman raised her arms up and arched her wings through the air. Michel scurried over to her, and looked up at the statue. Philippe looked with wide eyes.

Brighter than anything else in the garden, as red as roses or a sunset, birds flitted over the statue's hands.

"She's not going catch them like that," said Michel. Philippe giggled, and started to laugh, and Michel joined him. The laughter rang from the stones. All about, things stilled, even the fish in the pond, and from statuary and all the carvings on the house, eyes looked at them, and the house glowered.

The laughter carried out of the garden, all the same, and across the way where schoolgirls walked to Queen Hesione's school and talked of what they would have worn to Queen Shulamith's ball, and how it would have looked in her enchanted mirrors, to an open window across the way, where Reinette, frowning, looked up from her jewelry.

"I had thought this quarter held no children," she said, snipping out each word. "I had thought it had been chosen for that."

"There weren't," said Augusta. "It had been. But such things happen—Your Majesty."

Reinette scowled and sat back. That was no tone to take to the queen, even if you were her mother. She picked up a string of pearls, and then let it dribble through her fingers. Not that her mother would listen. It seemed unregal to scold, especially to no effect. She was a queen and not a fishwife.

"You must concentrate on finding a suitable bridegroom," said Augusta. "There are too many nobles here. They will try as earnestly as any fool back home to lure you into an unequal match, and here they have many more ways to hide their birth."

As bad as Queen Lenore was, thought Reinette. "I must prepare, then, and so it is time to go for ribbons."

Augusta paused, and Reinette smiled. For once she had taken her aback.

"It's—look at the clouds," said Augusta. "It will *rain*."

"You talk as if I would go on *foot*, like some thread-bare princess who slaves in a kitchen," said Reinette. "I will go in the carriage, of course, and properly attended. I know that no one respects royalty who do not keep proper state. By the same token, I can hardly be so *countri-fied* as to wear ribbons from home."

She swept off, calling for servants. They leapt up from their chatter—all about this nonsense about an invasion or some queen's ball. She didn't pay them to prattle about such commonplaces. Her commands snapped out, and they flew for her mantle, to harness the horses, to lead out her carriage.

When it glittered before the house, with the horses in their golden harness, Augusta stood by the front door, her mantle over her shoulders, her face as calm as though she had proposed the expedition.

Reinette nodded to her. It would hardly do to leave her behind. For all the perils of matrimony, whether an equal match or an inferior one (since she had no superiors to wed), at least no one would claim she need her mother to chaperon her once she married. Until then, a queen could not go so unattended as a milkmaid.

Reinette climbed into the carriage on her own and settled on the purple velvet of the seats. The groom helped Augusta up after her. Reinette cast her a sidelong glance. That, after all, had long been Augusta's aim: to make her daughter the queen, and so her superior.

The carriage lumbered off and down the narrow streets. It rose up the slope to High Street, and Alixandre, over tea, said, "Why, there she is." As the others glanced, "The carriage is that of Queen Reinette. Queen Lenore's niece."

"Oh, yes," said Blanca, without rising to look out the window. "Queen Lenore was truly foolish to have given birth to a bear. Now she is merely the queen dowager, and not the queen mother."

Ida shook her head, pouring more tea. She reached for the honey. "I don't imagine that there was actually a law against a bear succeeding."

Alixandre snorted. "Hardly needs to be one." Her gaze went back to the carriage. It rolled on, far beneath them, toward the river, through a welter of towering buildings that loomed over it with unreadable windows looking down but reflecting only the scene before them.

Augusta gave those windows a glance before she said, "I can not imagine that this is the quickest route. Not when we had to go up so high. . . ."

"But look," said Reinette, "there is the river."

Wider than some lakes she had seen, the river glinted back the sky's gray, and in the shadow of the waves, rolled darkly along. One could hardly mistake the shop, not with all the carriages by it, and the liveried grooms playing at dice, and the gentlemen talking of how their wives, or daughters, or sweethearts, shopped. In fact—Reinette's eyes narrowed—she could hardly mistake some of those gentlemen. Her mouth felt sour. Nobles who fled to the City of Exiles as if they had reason to fear her. . . .

When the carriage stopped, and the groom opened the door, Reinette sat still. She almost wished she had dressed more regally, but retreating home would hardly impress them. The groom held out his hand, and Reinette took it to descend.

At least they recognized her. Both Luc and Silvio bowed.

Reinette smiled. "How odd to find you here. I had not thought that either of you had any reason to flee my kingdom—nor that you were such fops and dandies as to shop here."

"Here?" said Silvio. He straightened, as if about to put his hand to his sword. "We are escorting a goddaughter of my mother's cousin."

"But then," said Reinette, "such a task makes your flight more puzzling." She took out her fan to fan herself and hide half her face while she studied them. "Surely you know you could not have fallen into your godmother's power, letting her assign you such feats, if you had remained home."

Silvio shrugged. "But, Your Majesty, we were chased from your kingdom—by—by our own youth and love of adventure! You must concede that the marvels here allure young men."

"Our fathers drive us into exile," said Luc, "so we will disgrace ourselves in foreign lands rather than where their reputations will suffer." His smile, unsurprisingly, did not reach his eyes; he had mastered that much of being a courtier.

"I know that young men love adventure," said Reinette. "That is why they go to the forests to hunt."

"Only some of them," said Luc. "Some of us are such fops and flirts that we can not bear such isolation." He bowed again. "Doubtlessly, Your Majesty, we will see you in all your finery at the city's festivities."

"And this store shall provide them to us," said Augusta, stepping forward. Her eyes were narrowed, and her mouth pursed. Reinette scowled, but walked with her, and Augusta spat, "Slanging in the street like a fishwife! They will think *nothing* of you."

Reinette gave her a baleful glance—a queen should not have to care what such passers-by thought—and hurried on, into the store. Cloth and ribbons burst to either side, and a slim brown woman, bending like a river reed, looked up.

"Ah—Queen Reinette, is it not?" She smiled, blandly. "I am sure we can find ribbons to please a queen here."

Another woman, her brown hair loose in curls about her shoulder, came toward the door, bearing a basket on her arm. Reinette walked by her without a glance, and Henrietta walked on, to Silvio and Luc.

"Found all you wanted?" said Luc.

"Found everything that we need," said Henrietta, her mouth set in sour lines. "Lady Maude would never consent to buying more than we need for the parties."

Luc rolled his eyes, but Henriette's sour expression did not change. They started up the streets.

"And I would not buy a thread more than we need. She has the maids do *some* of the work, but Lady Marjorie and I have to sew, and sew, and sew. As if some queen mother would decide that the woman who sewed the best would be her daughter-in-law." She arched her neck, and her hair fell free. "Worse today. We are all ready for Queen Shulamith's ball, but she *will* say that it will rain today, and so Lady Marjorie and I must *stick* to our sewing."

"Lady Marjorie," said Luc. "Did you know her before she came here?"

Henrietta slowly straightened and looked at him, narrowing her eyes. "No. I did not." After a minute, she said, "Do you have cousins or unmarried uncles?"

She was quick to presume on invitations to dance. "Silvio's a cousin," Luc said.

Her mouth pursed, and they walked up the street in silence. Silvio deliberately stepped behind Henrietta's back and, casting a sidelong glance at her, cocked an eyebrow at Luc.

Luc shrugged. He had done nothing to encourage her, at any rate, and they could deliver her back to Lady Maude. It was better here, at least, than at home, where the court ladies of their kin would have them running errands day and night. It would be worse there when Queen Reinette secured her coronation, and no one could escape her whims.

Down a cross-street ran a brown little man, barely reaching the height of Luc's shoulder. He drew a deep breath at the crossroads, glancing about as if to be sure enough people gawked at him.

"The invasion! The invasion's come!"

"The invasion!" It echoed all about. Apprentices looked up from their work, shopkeepers from their counters, vendors from their sales, and Luc's mouth pursed. At the shop next to them, the three daughters begged, and finally, their father let them go.

"Really," said the shopkeeper, "it's not likely that people will go shopping now."

"Really," said Henrietta, pulling her skirt aside as a shopkeeper's daughters hurried by her, "they act as if it's never happened before."

"What," said Luc, "you don't want to go?"

Henrietta's mouth pursed. "Once you've seen one of them, you've seen them all."

"You've seen one before?" said Silvio. "When was the last one? I would have thought you were too young."

Henrietta looked away.

At least, Maude's house lay, visible, ahead, thought Luc. He strode on. Silvio matched his pace, and Henrietta had to hurry to keep up.

With only the briefest thanks, she darted inside, without an invitation in or a glance back. Luc let his breath out.

"Cousins," said Silvio gloomily. He turned away, to where people streamed through the streets. His smile twitched at his mouth. "Then, of course, there's the invasion."

Without another word, they went up the street. Luc calculated buildings and roofs; they were not close to the gates, and a position to see all would not be easy to find in the crowd.

Two women came down the street, against the flow: Marjorie, looking harried, and a maidservant. Luc walked toward them, and Marjorie started.

"Good morning—what is this all?" She turned her hazel eyes—so mismatched with her black hair—toward him. "An invasion? They act more like a troupe has come to the city. And not any old troupe—one with a—" Her hand swept the air. "—entire company of dancing bears with a band to play for them, and talking parrots, and seventeen magicians without peer—not an army!"

Luc smiled. Closer than she knew.

"It's not like they all want to stare at the uniforms. There's only so much you can do with cloth and braid and you can see it on the street every day."

"Yes, it's an invasion," said Luc. No doubt Marjorie could see that no one lugged such treasures as they could carry, seeking to escape. Certainly, no one looked frightened except the smallest of children, and them at the tumult. He doubted his ability to explain it to her. And Silvio looked impatient.

"I was visiting Johanna—she's a cousin who lives here, but poor and ailing—" She pulled back her loose hair from her face. "With all this commotion, she has to rest." She looked back at Luc. "Even Johanna wasn't frightened, and she *couldn't* flee. What is happening?"

Luc drew a deep breath. "Would you like to see?"

The maidservant looked over, sharply. "How could you? It's dangerous—"

Silvio's shout of laughter cut her off.

Marjorie smiled. "I would like to." As soon as Luc held out his arm, she stepped forward to take it. Luc calculated buildings and roofs again. He could not take Marjorie everywhere where his own feet could bear him.

"This is absurd," said the maidservant.

"Of course," said Silvio. "Gabbing while everyone else is going to see—it is far from the most important thing happening in the city, but it is unquestionably the one with the best spectacle—but we shall see nothing, even if we arrive in time, because we will have no position to do it from." He walked off, briskly, and Luc and Marjorie followed. The maidservant scurried after.

"Everyone is fascinated," said Marjorie, her voice low. "How often does this happen, to entrance us all when it does?"

Luc felt his mouth twitch, and confessed, "This is the first time since I've been here. But they say you haven't really been to the City if you have not seen an invasion."

"It can't—they wouldn't—the kings would not have held their parleys here if it were so dangerous."

"Oh no," said Luc. "The invasions only really started after this started to be the city of exiles. But dangerous?"

"Here's a good way," called Silvio, drawing eyes all about. But when the crowd saw how he gestured at a gray alley, scarcely large enough for a single person, most hurried along on the road. Luc walked up. The alleyway twisted ahead of them.

"You're up to some mischief, I know," said the maidservant, wrathfully.

"Only seeing the invasion," said Luc. He had to loose Marjorie's arm for them to hurry through the alleyway, with Marjorie following Silvio, and the maidservant scurried after them all. The walls to either side towered over them—featureless, with no windows as high as they went—and the alley quickly turned into a long flight of narrow stairs, turning here and there so they could not see its height. The top of the walls never seemed to be any closer; between the two, they could see only scraps of cloud. They climbed, and climbed, and an arch bore a passageway overhead, with tiny windows looking down.

"Bet you that can see the invasion from the windows," said Silvio, "but there's no easy way there. Not like—" He strode up seven steps, and about a turn. His voice filled with satisfaction, he said, "Not like this."

Marjorie climbed. About the turn, a wall towered, but it held an arched doorway, and beyond, a balcony from which they could see buildings and clouds. Silvio smiled and handed her through.

From the balcony, the gates were clear to be seen: enormous, high enough to admit an elephant, built of oak so old as to be black, and bound with wrought iron. They opened on the square, now devoid of people. A few birds twittered on the flagstones, pecking here and there at crumbs, flitting about as if they watched the gates. All the stores had put up heavy shutters on their windows, and their doors were shut—heavy oaken doors, doubtlessly bolted. She had seen prisons with doors less secure.

Marjorie let her breath out. Shutters barred the second story windows, and even the third, but the higher windows had people leaning out, and crowds filled the roofs and murmured. Like people expecting a grand parade. With dancing bears—no, they had seen dancing bears on the street. With dancing lions and unicorns.

And there were no barriers set up on any street in.

Marjorie's eyes went back to the gate. No guards, even, stood there.

Luc came up beside her. His hand came up, across her back, to touch her other elbow, and Marjorie looked down at her hands. Muttering ferociously, the maidservant settled by the stairs. Silvio leaned against the balcony.

Marjorie tilted her head to one side. "How many invasions have you seen?" she said to the maidservant.

The maidservant shifted and muttered something about, "Too many."

A great thundering note shook the gate. After a minute, it creaked open. With such twittering cries that they filled the air with noise, the birds leapt upward, their wings beating as they flew for the roofs. A cloud of feathers spread, and sunlight shone through the wings, making the birds luminous.

The gate continued to open, revealing nothing behind it.

"Magic," said Silvio as the gates moved steadily. "More elegant than a battering ram, I suppose."

"Depends on the magic, by all accounts," said Luc.

Marjorie noted what they said, to sound less like a fool at the next ball.

Fully open, the gates admitted files of soldiers, each of them gleaming in blue with gold braid, their polished guns held ready. Their officers, bearing swords, rode on prancing, eager horses, every one of them a fine black.

"Folly," said Silvio, his voice dry. "Matching horses like that is for show, not for war. Their commanders should know that the City is not to be overawed."

"But," said Marjorie, "it is to be taken by force?"

Silvio blinked, and Luc laughed.

"She has you there. Once they choose to invade, it's not a question of prudence or folly, but a choice of follies."

She looked back at the folly in the square. From this distance, she could not see whether the soldiers were taken aback by the emptiness that greeted them. Not until companies had marched within did anyone in the army show any hesitation. An officer shouted a demand for surrender. After a moment, he shouted that the city had always fallen within the borders of the country. She could not make out the name he used. She supposed it did not matter.

Laughter rose from windows all about. Even Luc and Silvio smiled.

Marjorie stirred a little. The officer's face, turned upward, moved as if he were looking for something. "Why doesn't he *look* at them?"

"He can't hear them," said Luc. "Or see them."

"All part of the magic," said Silvio, merrily. "See how he doesn't threaten to *besiege* the city, cutting off our food—and the chances of exiled kings to come here and hide."

Marjorie's mouth curved, a little, but smoothed itself back out. The soldiers shouted taunts; raucous as they were, they lost something, dying out before they echoed far through the streets. Officers marched them on, down streets that seemed narrower, and more dingy and gray, than they had moments earlier.

Marjorie shivered. Luc's arm tightened about her, and she was glad of the warmth.

The streets had been level, she had seen that, but now, the soldiers marched downwards. Streets grew narrower beneath her gaze. Buildings loomed about the men, as tall as the tallest she had seen in the city, or taller. She could see only those who had marched down streets giving her a clear view, away from her. Shadows fell on them. In the begrimed streets, the uniforms no longer shone; the blue seemed almost gray. Streets twisted before them, like a labyrinth, and they turned corners, and were gone.

"I wonder if they can still see them, elsewhere," said Luc.

Marjorie shuddered. "It's horrible, horrible."

Silvio gave her a sideways glance.

"It's an invasion," said Luc. "What they intended—"

Marjorie looked at him. "I doubt their king, or even any of their princes, was one of those gallant officers."

Luc shifted. "They spoke of their country, not their kingdom. Probably some republic trying to seize run-away royalty."

Marjorie swept the air with her hand. "Some president or consul or what have you then—was not one of those gallant officers. I doubt that many soldiers had any choice."

"Dying on the battlefield wouldn't have given them a choice," said Luc. "Neither would their foes' dying there."

Silvio snorted. "Adventure is one thing," he said, "but I have no wish to fight off one of those armies."

Marjorie drew a deep breath, turning away from the balcony. The maid looked up hopefully. Marjorie looked at the stairs, but she said, "Will they vanish?"

"There are tales of bedraggled soldiers making a wild appearance at this party or that," said Luc.

"Going to Queen Shulamith's ball?" said Silvio.

Marjorie blinked. "Is it likely?"

"Possible," said Luc. "Not likely." His mouth twisted. "Certainly no more likely than one or two appearing in Lady Maude's garden."

Laughter suddenly echoed, nearby. Two little boys, in black clothing but bright faced, ran down the balcony. Luc started down the stairs
again, and they left the balcony to Michel and Philippe, running along
in delight, glad to be free and glad to have seen the soldiers utterly baffled.

"Never escape!" said Philippe, gleefully.

"Never," said Michel, glad that they had listened to the tales on the
street of the invasion. They reached the end of the balcony and started
down the stairs there. Better than that nasty old house. The streets below were filled with laughing people, rejoicing in their escape.

"Amazing that any of them try it," called one old man, and Michel
wandered along the streets with Philippe, and told him about even bigger and bolder soldiers back home, who wore uniforms of purple and
gold, much more fitting than the blue these ones wore.

They reached a corner, and Michel stopped, trying to ponder
which way to go. He had heard that the city had bad places in it, and he
had never seen this place before.

"Where are we going, Michel?" said Philippe.

"Home," said Michel, without hesitation, but he did not move.

"Home, of course," said a deep, disapproving voice, from far over
their heads. Michel slowly looked up. Ash-colored, tall and thin like
chimney, a man he had never seen before looked down at them with
eyes as black as soot. "You will go home at once." Lean hands with fingers like bone came down to take them each by hand. "After all the
trouble you brought your great-great-grandfather, to go and vanish like
that."

Michel did not quite follow their path through the streets. The
man strode along, his legs so long that Michel and Philippe had to
scramble to keep up, and panted for breath without his having pity on
them. The buildings seemed paler and more drab than any they had
seen before. None of them had so much as a window box of flowers, he
could barely tell them apart, the people wore dingy clothing and never

looked up from the flagstones, and even trying to remember the turns made Michel dizzy.

The first thing he recognized was the gate of his great-great-grandfather's house, and though he hated it again on sight, he walked toward it. He did not know what the tall, thin man could do.

Inside the gate, Michel and Philippe walked toward the door. Behind them, the tall, thin man latched the gate, and then Philippe gasped.

"Where did he go?"

Michel frowned and looked about. The man had latched the gate from the inside, he had seen it, but the garden held no trace of him. He grabbed Philippe's hand. "Let's go inside."

The corridors seemed placid, as if their outing had given them time to calm themselves. They did not let go of each other's hands, wandering along them.

"We got to the invasion," said Philippe. He peered down a side corridor. "And *everyone*'s going to Queen Shulamith's ball."

Not boys and girls, thought Michel. Even big boys and girls, and they were still little.

The light that came through the windows ahead left most of the white-washed corridor in shadow; they stood in the gloom.

Philippe rubbed his nose. "The bear lady might be back in the square. With the bear."

With that thought, they ran up the stairs and out on the balcony to look. The woman was indeed there, her scarlet skirt flaring as she and the bear moved through a country dance. Philippe laughed.

"What impudent children you are," said a woman. Michel turned. A thin, short woman, barely taller than Michel, stood in the door to the balcony, which they had left open behind them. Her nose flared, and she walked briskly forward, to take them by the arm and draw them back inside. "Letting drafts into the house like that." She shut the door behind them. And then she was gone as the man had gone.

Michel drew his breath in and let it out. He should have watched the woman by the pool.

He turned to Philippe and said, "We will go to Queen Shulamith's ball." And then he looked about for a window, and they went to watch the bear's dancing through it.

The woman and bear pirouetted through a dainty dance, and coins clattered around them. Gemma kept a careful eye on the money; that kept her face down, hiding her expression. Once inside the ball, she could learn the truth of the mirrors, and it was so close she could taste it—but any noble might be able to keep her out, if he thought she was up to something, or even if he just took a distaste to her. Queen Shulamith would hardly offend a guest of noble blood for the sake of a street entertainer. Who really was of common blood, if it came to that.

With the last measure, Gemma turned to curtsy, far more gracefully than the bear bowed. But—her mouth twisted—it was the bear's bow that brought applause, albeit with laughter and more coins. She stooped to gather up the coinage. Someone would wonder, if she were careless about her pay. Then having gathered it all, she headed toward the park. And admitted to herself that they might need the money as well.

They walked down an almost empty street when the bear growled, "Dancing all day, and then at the ball—"

Gemma glanced at housewives gossiping about a doorway. Did the bear *want* to give them something to gossip about?

"You've done it before," she said, not looking at the bear. "And with a prospect this close, you would be a fool to risk it."

"We don't even know if Queen Shulamith's mirrors will help." Sounding sullen and malcontent.

"Nothing else in the city will, and we will know soon enough," said Gemma. When a handful of schoolgirls slipped out of a side road and chattered on their way to the park, Gemma thanked God. She hurried to keep up with them, and the bear lumbered along, holding its tongue.

If only this would work, the bear would forgive her.

One schoolgirl glanced scornfully over her shoulder, as if disdaining the very thought of watching a dancing bear, so commonplace. Gemma's mouth twitched. At the gate to the park, she took the fork that led to the great lawns. Few people looked at her, and none drew near, but she set up as if she expected a crowd, or as if every coin she might draw was inestimably precious. And then, setting the magic playing the music, she began to dance on the lawn.

The bear lumbered into the measures as if they had not quarreled on the way, and Gemma turned, her skirt swirling. An orange butterfly hung on the air, as if she had shed it. She smiled and turned into the dance, and saw two more butterflies, the sunlight passing through their orange wings and making them glow.

The music held her; she danced on. And perhaps, it was the dance that brought them, as butterfly after butterfly flew up from the ground or in from the lawn and flitted and glowed about them. The bear hesitated now and again, and Gemma did not know how she kept to her step; it was like dancing in the heart of a gemstone.

The music stopped. Gemma stood, panting. Butterflies flew up, and down, and slowly fluttered away, the cloud dispersing over the park. Gemma watched them go. And she had not drawn watchers. There would be no coin. And, with her heart pattering from more than the dance, she did not care what conclusions anyone would draw. Queen Shulamith wanted her at the ball, and she needed nothing else. She gathered up everything again, and started to walk about the park. In the silence, the bear lumbered along with her, down the long paths, under willows by a lake, and up into a corner where oaks stood before the buildings that edged the park.

Gentlemen had gathered by that gate, and Gemma hesitated. Best not to go that far, and tempt fate. After a moment, she stepped closer to the bear. It did not growl, but its shoulders bunched, and it would growl the moment it thought her threatened. Which would tempt those young men. Like every nobleman in the city, they wore swords, and they looked young enough to wish to use them and show their bravery. It was not as if she could take them to court for killing her bear.

She let her breath out. When they were so close—she looked about, for the best path away. They had to start for the ball soon.

A woman shrieked. Gemma's head whipped around. A woman staggered out of an alleyway, into the park. In a fine golden gown—which showed a little dirt, but was not tattered at all. No one followed her out, but her face was pale as bone, color utterly drained form her lips.

"Gentlemen!" Reinette's voice tried to ring, but faltered. "Gentlemen! There are soldiers from the invasion—" She waved back at the alleyway. "They are chasing me!" She stared from face to face. Surely no man of common blood would dare carry a sword, and no man of noble blood would stand aside while riffraff menaced a queen, and above all else a young and lovely queen.

But they did not move—

They even eyed her as she were no more than the dancing girl with her bear.

"Yeah," said one man. "We can hear the footsteps." And at that they all laughed. Some of them eyed her with scorn.

"Ask the bear," shouted another. He waved back at it, standing next to that black-haired woman, the entertainer. "A great fierce bear like that would protect you better."

The woman stepped back. "He must go and dance at Queen Shulamith's ball." She scurried off, without a glance back, her red skirt swirling. The bear lumbered along, and Reinette stared after her, with narrowed eyes. Such impudence.

She remembered the soldiers and started. Looking back, she could not see them, but she could never mistake those blue uniforms, with their gold braid, even torn and filthy and bloodied. She shuddered and fled. When they burst out, the soldiers would find those *gentlemen*, and the soldiers had been too wild and uncaring about whom they attacked to chase after her while they had such foes before them.

And she would never ever—even to hide from her mother—leave the house again without proper state. She drew her breath in and let it out. She would relegate her mother *somewhere*. A tower where they brought up the food by basket might be secure enough. As for reason, she could cook up something. Accuse her of treason, at need. Augusta fought to make her queen. Let her learn that she succeeded, and her daughter would be *queen*. And never have to suffer such insolence again. Neither from *gentlemen* nor from street dancers.

She stalked off, or tried to; she could not keep her path straight. The streets clamored with people. Children ran before her as if they could not imagine caring who she was—children in apprentice's smocks, or with dirty faces and torn clothes.

Reinette looked away, but she was not near enough a wall to block out such sights. And she had come to find a bridegroom here! Perhaps even among those rascals who jeered at her plight! Her mouth tightened. She would never wed. She would remain single forever, and it would serve her kingdom right if her death left them scrambling for an heir. The only reason they supported her claim enough to win her a coronation was their own rivalries: they could not support a single pretender to put her down.

She stormed up the stairs into the house. Servants exclaimed and whirled about, bearing her off like a breeze taking up leaves. Up in her chambers, the women, full of shock and concern, took off her gown to replace it and fussed over whether it could be repaired at all, and over her bruises. Well enough, Reinette thought, begrudgingly. Even in this city, people occasionally knew the respect owed to royalty—

The shatter of glass broke into her thoughts.

Reinette blinked and cast her gaze about. Across the room, a woman—one of the clumsy oafs—cringed over a broken perfume bottle.

Moments later, the room rang from the slap, and Reinette's hand stung. "Go," she spat. "Go at once. You are no longer in my service." She whirled away. "Where is the captain of my guard?"

They fluttered, some of them fleeing and saying that he must know that she would need him, he would be ready to serve her, they would just find him. . . .

He came, a minute later. He looked rather gray, but he bowed, and straightened for her orders.

She fought down a twitch of her lip. They knew her to be just; and she knew that she had evaded his protection. He had no right to act as if she would dismiss him. But if he knew her so poorly, she would not betray her mood to him.

"The woman who dances with the bear in the streets—the black-haired woman, wears a fiery red dress."

The captain nodded.

"She mocked me." Reinette turned a little. "She mocked me this day, and *you* must see to it that she does not run off and dance at Queen Shulamith's ball as if such street tatterdemalions could speak to—"

She cut off her words before she sounded more of a fishwife than she already had. The captain bowed. She let her breath and hoped he did not fall her as badly as that maidservant, as he left the room.

He strode more quickly as soon as he left the room—past the room where other maid servants whispered encouragement to the dismissed one, about how the city held many nobles from their kingdom, she was certain to find a place—and once in the guards' quarters, he shouted for his men and sent them out on the streets. Queen Shulamith's ball—as if the woman, like any entertainer, would not arrive early, long before the ball began.

If they did not find her—he wondered if the men would return to warn him, so that he would know not to return to Queen Reinette's house, himself.

But one, scarcely more than a boy, came running back, over the cobblestones, with the news that they had seen this Gemma walking with her bear toward Queen Shulamith's palace.

"Good," said the captain. A woman foolish enough to mock a queen might indeed be foolish enough to walk so late to the ball. And in the streets of this city, no more safe than any other—less safe than some. He loosened his sword in its scabbard, and summoned the rest to follow him as they walked out on the street. Servants running with packages took one glance at them and darted from their way. Vendors fell silent and pulled into the shelter of an alleyway. Even a querulous old man, walking with a cane and holding the arm of his granddaughter, stopped his rambling long enough to see them, and not walk in their way.

The noise of their footsteps drew Gemma's attention. She glanced over her shoulder, even as the captain saw her and ordered his men to move out. She could see how they eyed her.

The bear snarled, fiercely.

"You can not fight them all," said Gemma. "Run on." She grabbed her skirts, and ran. After a moment, the bear lumbered into a run: awkward, but fearfully fast. The soldiers shouted and ran after. Someone bellowed at them, "What are you doing?" but the ringing footsteps did not hesitate, and no one, of course, stood in the way of armed men.

She ran so quickly that her thoughts were laggard and took minutes to realize that they wore the livery of that woman—who must have taken offense. Her mouth tightened. She had to escape; they would not decide she was too much of a bother to chase.

Not the shops, thought Gemma. No shopkeeper could stand against soldiers. She wished she knew the alleyways here, but she could be trapped as well as escape through one, if she picked the wrong one. The house of nobles stood ahead. The soldiers would not dare—but they shouted and ran after her into those streets. Then, no gentlemen stood about to stop them. . . .

A garden gate opened ahead of her. A black-haired young woman, in green brocade, gestured at her, and Gemma did not hesitate. Especially when the woman was too finely gowned to be a servant.

"Stop her!" bellowed from behind, but Gemma and the bear slid within. The woman—the Lady Marjorie, she had been at the ball—slammed the gate shut and bolted it. A good solid bolt, on a heavy iron gate. The soldiers would have to break through that. If they dared. And if there were no enchantments on it to complicate even that. Gemma stood, panting—the bear was breathing hard itself.

"Come," said Marjorie, and for all that her legs ached, Gemma did not argue as the woman led her and the bear deeper in a rose garden. Flowers brushed their petals against them, red and pink and yellow.

"*Marjorie!*"

Lady Maude towered in the gap between two bushes heavy with blood-red roses, and eyed Marjorie up and down. "When you *knew* your father's wishes—and you have made yourself unfit for the ball!"

Marjorie gaped. She looked at herself, and realized that somehow in that flight, she had torn her sleeve. She looked miserably at it. She would, she supposed, have done the same thing whatever she had known would come of it, but to have accidentally—she felt a fool.

"Perhaps you should address yourself to *sewing*," said Lady Maude. "Perhaps you might manage to make yourself presentable for the ball—in time." She turned, her violet skirts swirling about her, and stalked off.

Certainly not in time, thought Marjorie, miserably. She could not sew well enough to make the tear invisible, and Lady Maude would require it.

She felt a hand on her arm. "Come," said Gemma. "Come deeper into the garden."

Marjorie hesitated, and then took a few steps with her.

Gemma turned to the bear as she walked. "*You*, stay here."

The bear looked at her for a moment, and sat down on its haunches. Gemma whirled Marjorie away, to where the rose bushes hid them from all, and a small bench sat under an arbor of yellow roses.

Gemma said, "Now, take your gown off."

Marjorie eyed her, but then, she had her shift on, under it, and a woman who could make a bear dance like that must be truly odd. Carefully, she unlaced and shed the gown. Then she spread it on the bench. If Gemma could do something about the tear. . . .

Gemma raised her hands and started to move them, swifter and more gracefully than when she danced—and more oddly, too. After a moment, a petal flew off the rose bushes, then, another, and another. They swarmed over the woman, and then Gemma brought her hands down, and the petals flooded over Marjorie, as ticklish as the brush of a bee's wings. But these settled and formed, and Marjorie found herself staring down at an elegant gown, glowing yellow. She moved, hesitantly.

"It will hold," said Gemma. "As good as any woven fabric. Longer than many."

Marjorie eyed the poppy-red of Gemma's skirts, and Gemma smiled. Marjorie let her breath out and took up the brocade gown. With time, she could sew the tiny, careful stitches that would let her wear the gown again, at another ball. For now, before the ball—

"Come with me. Bring your bear."

Gemma's mouth twisted.

At their approach, the bear looked up, and looked as surprised as that furry maw could manage. It lumbered to its feet. Marjorie led them, quickly, through the garden, to a little back gate, and Gemma breathed a sigh of relief. She and the bear walked quickly down the back alleyways to the barn.

"I—" said the bear. "We have to get to the ball."

She had never heard him nervous before. Certainly never so nervous. "I know. Therefore, I will do nothing elaborate. We shall have to run some risks."

She considered the streets a minute. They could choose their path as well. "Stand still," she said, and murmured through a spell. "That will—obfuscate us. They will not know us, if they do not see much of us." She let her breath out. "Come. We must go *now*. The route will be longer."

The bear ambled along, but when she turned down to the river, it slowed for a moment, and then walked closer to her. Every now and again, she felt the brush of his rough fur against her skirts.

"Turn here, by the bridge," she whispered, and stopped. Firelight gilded the bridge's stones. She could not see the fire itself or, worse, who stood about it.

She had walked boldly enough with the bear, through all the roads that had brought them to the city, and all streets that had borne them through it. She walked on. The bear's pace had not slowed; she wondered if he had even noticed her hesitation.

A shrill pipe sounded, and a tune sprung up. A dancing tune, and her feet began to ache already. Gemma set her mouth and walked on, down the stairs. After this night, she could declare herself sick of dancing and never do it again.

A woman danced, a black form against the orange flare of the fire, and nearly as graceful and supple as the flames themselves, dancing in river breezes.

If it hadn't been for the bear, thought Gemma, her own dancing would never have drawn such coins. She kept on walking.

But as she reached the last stair, the music stopped. She looked up. The firelight fell on the face of the dancer—Esmeralda's face.

"Ah," she called. "The dancing woman, with the dancing bear."

Gemma swallowed.

Esmeralda turned again, her skirts swirling. "Here's to hoping that you find your way back to being a fine lady."

Gemma hurried by. The bear eyed them as it clumped on, and Gemma thought of putting a hand to its head, but it did not turn to them. They vanished into an alleyway, and Gemma hurried along it.

She had reckoned the streets rightly. They came out next to Queen Shulamith's house. The first carriages had arrived, and the guests descending in glitter. A vendor in the street hawked delicate little butterflies, red, orange, or blue, for the fine ladies to wear in their hair.

Gemma let her breath out. It was well that Queen Shulamith wanted them to come not so early in the ball. She edged toward the doorway.

A carriage drew out, and Lady Maude swept out. Though arrayed with diamonds on blue, she looked as if she had bitten something sour. Gemma stopped. Moments later, a young woman with curly brown hair came out, and then, black-haired, in a yellow gown, Marjorie appeared. Perhaps she should have chosen a different rose bush; the color was not perfectly for her hair, but—

"At least she kept her word about letting her," Gemma murmured, and went inside. The obfuscation spell should work until she addressed the queen, and the arriving guests did indeed notice no more of either of them than a bit from the corner of their eyes. Marjorie thought she saw a flick of red, but though she knew Gemma would appear to entertain them, she could not be sure that it was the woman's skirt. She would have to wait to learn that the woman was well—and her bear, too.

In Lady Maude's wake, she swept up the stairs toward the doors. Lady Maude would certainly have no reason to complain of her behavior at the ball. Other guests clumped about the door. Her gaze passed over them, noting this one and that, and faltered on Luc. He looked up and at her, smiled, and kissed his hand to her.

Feeling her cheeks heat, she looked down. She hurried after Lady Maude and Henrietta, to the doors, which revealed a chamber glittering. Candlelight filled it and reflected from the mirror opposite. She drew a deep breath and reminded herself of her manners: before all else, they had to greet Queen Shulamith.

The queen wore a dark indigo gown, not adorned with so much as pleating, and no jewelry, but even with her dark hair spread over her shoulders like any maid's, it was impossible to mistake her for anyone else. They glided into the line of guests, and Marjorie eyed the room as they waited, inching forward now and again. The ball had certainly drawn out the peacocks in the city. Even at balls, she had never seen such extravagance before, not in dyes, or ribbons, or jewelry.

And the mirror that covered the wall opposite to them—was that one of the mirrors of Queen Shulamith? She had heard tales of them—an unusual number of tales, even in this city, for something that no one had seen. Her gaze went over the reflected ball-goers, and then it stopped. Held prisoner by the image of a young woman in a yellow gown, her blond hair falling free over her shoulders. With that color hair, the yellow gown became her. Better than Marjorie's own gown of the same hue.

She stood next to Lady Maude and Henrietta, too—that blond, reflected maid.

Marjorie's hand jerked up to take up a lock of her own hair. Black, still dyed black. But in the mirror, the image had taken up a lock of blond hair and looked at it. . . .

Lady Maude's whisper broke in: "*Marjorie.*"

Even with all the fury in that name, Marjorie barely managed to look up. Henrietta pouted, Lady Maude glanced between her and the mirror and slowly looked appalled, and Queen Shulamith laughed, deep in her throat.

"I see," said the queen, "that you have seen the first of my mirrors." Then her gaze went past Marjorie, toward the door. Her eyebrows went up.

Among the throngs, drawing many gazes, two wan young boys. dressed in black, wriggled into the room—far too young to be up, let alone to attend a ball. They sidled along the wall, their faces and hair pale against their dark clothing, and when the taller saw that Queen Shulamith looked at him, he froze like a frightened fawn.

Mischief, thought Marjorie. And then—perhaps not—as all about her, ball-goers noted the boys, to shake their heads and whispered, she looked at the mirror. It could show the truth, it seemed.

It showed something looming over the boys. Too tall to be human, too pale, too *tenuous*—a ghost, thought Marjorie, with cruel clawed hands.

Then she realized that some of the staring ball-goers were staring at her. Lady Maude looked ready to strike her, Henrietta seemed about to sink into the floor, and others—others turned toward the mirror and paid Marjorie no more heed.

Shouts rose, of horror. Ball-goers, almost as pale as the reflection, pressed away from the mirrors, even toward the boys. The boys looked at the mirror and grew paler. The older one held the younger's hand tightly. The pale monster grew taller, thicker—more substantial? Marjorie felt the air growing colder about them, and after a moment, she blinked, trying to clear her vision. It did not help, nor did blinking again. The air seemed to have steeped in some dark miasma that dragged light into itself and swallowed it whole.

Silvio drew his sword.

Luc said, dryly, "That's not likely to work," but drew his own. All the adventure they had claimed to long for, right here in the ball. He strode forward, toward the boys; if only he could get between the boys and that ghostly monster.

"That will not work, gallant sir." Queen Shulamith's deep voice rang through the room. "They must go in there."

She pointed to another door. The ghost loomed, its hands descending toward the boys, and they grew almost as pale as it. The taller tried to take a step, and staggered.

Luc put up his sword, faster than he had known he could, and ran toward them. Footsteps echoed behind him, and when he reached and started to pick up the taller boy, Silvio appeared beside him to snatch the smaller. Neither boy struggled. Luc made the mistake of glancing at the mirror. The ghost loomed over their head. Its mouth gaped wide enough to swallow all four of them, and even its barely formed face could show anger.

Luc ran.

The ball-goers gaped and stared and did not move from the way. Some even pressed closer; Luc brushed by one portly lady, colliding with her gown, and left her exclaiming on his rudeness as he ran on, into the other room.

Fewer people had entered here already. Candles gleamed, and another mirror stood the length of the wall.

A few strides in, Luc stopped. The boy leaned on his shoulder as if too weak to straighten, but the mirror showed no monster—not even when Silvio followed with the other boy. He dragged in a deep breath. Abruptly, the air warmed and seemed to clear, so that all things sparkled again.

Marjorie slowly walked toward them. In the doorway, she called, "Bring them back here." Then she glanced at Queen Shulamith, who nodded.

Luc silently obeyed, and looked into the mirror on that side. It showed no sign of the monster, yet.

Marjorie touched the boy's hair. "Good evening," she whispered. "Who are you?"

"Michel," whispered the boy, and the ball-goers turned away, talking with great to-do about the monsters and the mirror, and how this would swamp anything else about the ball, and what a pity that such festivities would be marred by such a freakish event. Marjorie stepped closer. The smaller boy began to whimper against Silvio's shoulder, and Silvio scowled, but Michel straightened to look at him. "Philippe—" He pointed.

"Where do you come from?"

"From Great-great-grandfather's—" Michel wriggled, and Luc put him down. Silvio put down Philippe, and Michel grabbed his hand before inching through their tale of their dead parents, and how Great-great-grandfather had charge of them in his white house, and how they had left.

And Marjorie, bent to listen, pieced together the bits. And when they said their parents' names—"But you are my cousins!"

Michel blinked.

"You are my father's mother's brother's daughter's sons! I heard of how my cousin died, but I did not think of her sons." She straightened. And she had been so distraught that it meant staying with Maude. "It is clear that your care does not suit so elderly a gentleman. In the morning I will come to visit him, and offer to take you from his hands."

The boys' eyes looked like saucers. She would manage, Marjorie told herself. However much Lady Maude was offended, somehow she would manage to get these boys away from whatever haunted house that elderly *wretch* had inflicted on them.

"For now," she said, "I will send you home with servants."

"There is no need, Lady Marjorie." Queen Shulamith had come up so silently that she blinked in surprise; the woman's full skirts spread like the night sky, and Marjorie blinked, thinking she saw stars in the folds.

The queen smiled benignly on them all. "I will send a candleman with them myself. I have no wish for any guest of mine, however young, to have trouble returning to his home." And she bent to take the children's hands. With great wondering gazes, they took them.

"How did it work?" said Luc.

"Why, gallant sir, this mirror *sees* the truth." She nodded to the mirror showing Marjorie's pale hair. "And the mirror that you went to, *shows* the truth."

Marjorie fingered her dyed locks. She wondered whether she should go into that room, ever. This mirror showed what things really looked like. That mirror showed only what was visible, and made what was invisible vanish—because it showed no monster, there was no monster to be shown. She bit her lip. Lady Maude would be glad to shove her into it, she had no doubts. It would show her with black hair, and then the spell would not need renewing.

Queen Shulamith's smile deepened. "There is always that door." She nodded across the room. "There, the mirror both sees, and shows, the truth."

Marjorie turned and hurried toward it. The thick press made it worse than carrying the boys to the other room. Her skirts brushed those of many another lady, and some garlands lay strewn in her path. Ladies murmured behind their fans about such hoydenish behavior, and Luc looked after her.

"Will everything be such an uproar?" demanded a portly man, middle-aged, dressed in crimson velvet. "What sort of ball has such confusion? Will it last the length of it?"

"There is no need for it to last," said Queen Shulamith. "The mirrors can reveal only what is hidden." She smiled. "How many secrets can one ball hold?"

Her gaze went to the door that Marjorie had taken, and drew other gazes with it. The boys, wide-eyed, looked from her to the door and back. The murmurs did not perturb either her calm smile, or her steady gaze, until Marjorie reappeared.

She stood in the doorway and smiled radiantly. Her hair spread, golden, over her shoulders.

Lady Maude looked as if she had eaten a far too sour pickle, and Queen Shulamith stepped closer to her to murmur, "Certainly the gown is more pleasing with the true color. Why, she all but glows like the sun."

Lady Maude glared at her, but said nothing. About the ballroom, women edged toward the other room; some had fair hair, but most were dark. Marjorie herself walked across the room toward Lady Maude, and Luc slipped closer to her.

Gemma appeared in a doorway—not one of those with a mirror. She looked about until her gaze settled on Queen Shulamith, and the queen looked back. Then she curtsied, very deeply.

More deeply than to any other royalty or nobility in the city, thought Silvio.

Queen Shulamith turned, her dark skirt flowing out like the petals of a flower. "Listen," she called. "Come to see the dancing done by a bear and a woman."

"Come see how it's done," called Silvio. "Or the ladies will complain that you can not dance as well as a bear."

Laughter resounded. Queen Shulamith stepped aside with the boys. Luc closed the distance quickly, to offer Marjorie his arm. She smiled and took it. He felt almost light-headed—she looked so much more lovely with her hair its true shade—and they joined the throngs. The music struck up, and the ball-goers formed measures, and in their midst, Gemma danced with the bear, with a crowd gathered around her.

A shrill, imperious voice rang over all. "There she is!"

Guards appeared in the doorway, and in their center stood Reinette, flushed with anger and in an unbecoming violet gown. She glared at Gemma and the bear as if the room held no one else.

"Arrest her!" Her hoarse voice resounded. Her arm went up and pointed at the dancer.

The guards glanced about.

"Arrest her?" said Queen Shulamith, mildly. "At my ball?"

"You false queen!" raged Reinette. "You pretender!"

Marjorie's lips curved without her thinking of it. All about her muffled laughter showed that others also thought what havoc it would wreak on the city, to punish all who claimed false titles.

"And you shelter an impostor!" Reinette drew a deep breath, and her lip curled. "A wayfaring entertainer, indeed. That woman is a sorceress and a servant of Queen Lenore!" Reinette lowered her voice. "She can mean you no good. She can mean none of you any good at all."

"Oh, that tale," said a man with disgust.

"That *true* tale," said Reinette. "She was unspeakably insolent to me today. And a wizard revealed to me the truth. She would not have dared if she were not Queen Lenore's *pet*." She pointed, and her soldiers stared to move.

"What means this invasion?" called Marjorie. "Bringing armed forces within the city?"

"You are part and party to this treachery," said Reinette. "Sheltering that woman in your plot! Why else would any noble, let alone royal, have a care for a mere street entertainer?" She looked about. "There is a plot!"

The bear sat back on its haunches. "Yes, there is."

Silence rippled out, and faces went pale. Reinette took a step backward.

"But it is not Mistress Gemma's, pretender, false queen."

"You fool," whispered Gemma, her face paling—and the room so quiet that most of them heard her. "The danger."

The bear did not take its gaze from Reinette. "Where in all the laws does it decree that a bear, being the son of the king and queen, *can not* ascend the throne?"

"She has soldiers with her," said Gemma, despairing.

Reinette, her mouth set in mulish lines, took a step forward with her guards.

Silvio drew his sword; the sound rang in the room. Moments later, Luc did as well, Marjorie stepping away without a moment's thought, and other gentlemen—most young, some older, some completely old—and the ladies drew back, whispering among themselves, to leave the space clear. Gemma swallowed. To fight already. . . .

"Sir Bear," said Queen Shulamith, "what brings you to my humble ball?"

The bear bowed—as gracefully as it danced. "Your Majesty. I sought out the mirrors of your fame." It started to lumber off, and Gemma hurried beside it. The ladies, murmuring, parted only enough to let the two of them through. Marjorie felt her heart hammer, and glanced at her hair—still wheat-golden on her shoulders. Then she sidled toward the door. She did not reach it before a murmur spread outward. When she reached the doorway, a man, wrapped in a bearskin, knelt on the floor. A handsome young man. Her breath gushed out.

"Whatever does this mean?" whispered Henrietta.

"Why," said Marjorie dryly, pitching her voice to carry, "don't you notice how much he resembles Reinette? His cousin Reinette? He's the rightful king, the one who was born a bear."

Gemma, still very pale, said, "Queen Lenore's first born and second son were murdered by poison. She thought being born a bear would protect the child." She spread her hands. "She was right."

"You're an impostor," snarled Reinette, stalking through the crowd. With the guards to either hand, the crowd pulled back, and none of the gentlemen seemed ready to strike the first blow. Though they pulled closer to where the prince stood. Most of the dancers pulled farther away.

Gemma looked trapped. Marjorie sidled along the wall. For a moment, she glimpsed Maud turning red with rage, but she walked on until she came to the opposite side. There, she stepped out to take Gemma's hands and pull her back, toward the garden doors.

"Stay out of the way," she said in a low voice. "They will be able to fight more freely if the swords come into play." Then she realized how still the ballroom was, and how her voice carried. Reinette looked banefully at her.

"I don't want them to fight," said Gemma, with intensity. "The prince does not even have a sword—"

Silvio, with a flourish, drew off his mantle and offered to the prince. "You have the swords of loyal men, Your Highness."

"There is," said the prince, his voice still half growling, "no need for us to taint Queen Shulamith's ball. I shall withdraw and return to my native land to claim—"

"I will not have it!" shouted Reinette, raising her hands. Her guards looked at her, weighed their dangers, and drew their swords.

"Into the gardens, my men," said the prince. "I do not have so many of you that I can risk your lives."

Gemma grabbed Marjorie's hand. "Us first," she whispered. Marjorie scrambled with her out the doors.

The night was cool, and dew already formed on the grass. The ballroom's windows cast great golden squares of light across the lawn—making the shadows between them still darker, and hard to penetrate.

"The rose garden," said Marjorie.

"That will be a labyrinth," said Gemma.

Marjorie, remembering the invasion, said, "Exactly." Then she hurried toward the flowery scent. She glanced back. Gemma followed her, and then the prince, and his men.

The center, she told herself, as she walked between the first two hedges. From there, no doubt, they could escape to the city's labyrinthine streets—who would build a labyrinth without such mag-

ic?—and get inside some building where Reinette could not easily follow.

She turned right. That was usually the first turn, no one wished his
guests to be baffled and angry by the time they solved the maze. Her
confidence carried; the prince and the gentlemen followed her, down
this turn and that one and around and about.

The maze turned and branched and towered over her until Marjorie felt quite certain that she would have to confess to having gotten
them all lost—and instantly a square appeared before them, the grass
dew-laden but even, and rising toward a hillock. Marjorie ran toward
it before she remembered that she had seen no hillock from the windows—and after as well. However this hillock appeared here, even if it
had done so when they hurried through the maze, she had to see.

Such as she could. More shadows than light fell over the garden.
Here and there, lamplight glanced from swords or armor, but most of
the movement was dim and hard to make out. She swallowed. First of
all, to find a way out. . . .

"You are watching your plan from here?" said the prince, his voice
deep, as he came to stand beside her.

"My plan—but my hope, first," said Marjorie.

The prince glanced at her—she could the light glint from his
eye—but Gemma gasped, and pointed.

"That hedge," she said. "It moved."

The men gathered about them and watched the labyrinth in silence,
as the walls rose, and shifted, and the guards caught in them bellowed
in rage and tried to turn their swords in axes. Roses shifted about them.

Marjorie turned her face away. She did not want to see the roses
turn on the men.

Silvio called, "Look!" He pointed, with his left hand. A handful
of guards staggered from the maze onto the grass. The gentlemen all
braced themselves.

"I am the prince," the prince called. "The rightful prince. You all know how the queen's children died, one by one, until finally she gave birth to a bear—to shelter her last child from his enemies."

Silence fell. No one moved.

"Are you among those enemies?"

The guards bowed their heads, and turned to offer him the hilts of their swords. Gemma let her breath out slowly.

"This," she murmured, "has been a ramshackle and disorderly night. Hardly a ball at all."

The prince glanced sideways at her, and for a moment, she thought he looked fond.

"When was it not, my lady? From the hour when we left my mother's house, when were we not desperately pondering another way to take even the next step?"

Gemma let her breath out, slowly.

Marjorie whispered, "There ought to be a way out."

Gemma nodded, and looked down at the hedges. Then she blinked. "When did that happen?"

They all turned, one by one, as the first one stared and could not look away.

Queen Shulamith smiled benevolently upon them. Gemma wondered how much of the light could fall on her without seeming to shift through the air. The hedges, she knew, could move, but now they had moved to stand at either hand of the queen, leaving a wide and stately path.

"I would be a negligent hostess to let you scramble off now," she said. She inclined her head. "If you truly wish to leave, you may do so with dignity and grace."

The prince bowed, awkwardly. "Your Majesty, I fear I am not attired for a ball."

Her smile broadened. "Come within, come within—my Lady Marjorie, could you assist Lady Gemma within?"

Gemma remembered starting to descend, but did not quite follow all the rest until finally she stood among the ball-goers in her poppy-scarlet gown—a flower among the flowers of this field, no different from another—except that she could see the others gazing on her with more poison that she had ever seen in her life.

Some, she had to grant, were merely curious.

But one, aglitter with diamonds, descended on the two of them. Gemma frowned, thinking she should know her, but her face was so contorted with rage that she could not be recognized. At least on brief acquaintance—Marjorie stood still with recognition.

The woman surged close enough to whisper, "You little fool." She glared at Marjorie. "What were you *thinking*?"

Marjorie lifted her eyebrows, but Gemma thought she could see the strain. "Why, preventing discord at a ball. It's very unsuitable. A ball should have harmony. It was only courteous to our hostess the queen."

Lady Maud clapped her hand on Marjorie's arm. "You will have a chance to reconsider that in your chamber—"

"Her Majesty asked me to stay with Lady Gemma," said Marjorie.

"Lady Gemma?" Maud's lip curled.

"The prince said so," said Marjorie. "And you know that he is only not king because he is not crowned. Yet. The authority was his from the hour that his father died."

"When he pranced about the street for coins as a bear?"

"Yes," said Silvio, by her elbow. Maud turned her vicious expression on him, and he wondered whether she intended to make a spectacle of herself. But he had his commission from his king. He bowed to Gemma. "My lady, a new dance comes. Will you do me the honor of becoming my partner?"

Gemma hesitated. He had asked her once before, and not been a worse dancer than a bear. Perhaps she could even ask him what he had suspected, then. She nodded, and glanced at Marjorie, and saw Luc advancing to claim her hand, and Maud, sourly, withdrawing.

Was it not half the purpose of a ball to marry off the maidens? thought Gemma, feeling almost light-headed. She should be glad of a proper match for Marjorie, and with a man that the king would favor.

Music started, and the dance began. Silvio did not take her to the center of the floor, where all eyes would be on them, and she felt glad of it, though it was not so hard to remember, how to dance with a man instead of a bear. It had been easier in the stairway, out of sight.

"You dance even more gracefully than before," said Silvio.

"Perhaps your thoughts are less on your suspicions," said Gemma.

He sighed. "I must confess that my suspicions were too slight to claim any credit."

As the last measures ended, she found herself on the edge of the figure, and when she started to turn, the prince stood there and looked at her, smiling. Dressed better than most of the dancers—she would have been astounded to see such green velvet watching them on the street, and then expected gold from him.

Silvio bowed, and she remembered her curtsy. Then the prince bowed to her to ask the honor of the dance.

"I hope that I will master it in human form as well as in bear," said the prince.

"Will that be so difficult?" said Gemma.

He spread his hands. "You remember how I needed a servant to page through a book when I read it—my paws could not be trusted to turn it. There seems to be an art that I must master."

She curtsied again. "It would be my pleasure to aid you in mastery."

Silvio edged off, thinking he half-felt pleased that the prince did not act in love with her, even though the prince had to make a good alliance with his marriage, under any circumstances. He looked about for Luc and Marjorie, ready to claim Marjorie as a partner where Luc had to let her go.

The next dance was slow and stately, and most of the dancers left the floor, to stand where they could see the prince.

"You do not seem eager to gawk," said Marjorie.

"His Highness," said Silvio, "asked us to attend him when he returns to his kingdom."

"You—and Luc?"

Silvio nodded.

After a moment, Marjorie said, "I wish I could remain all hours and claim dances with you twain, but—I must rise earlier tomorrow."

Silvio's eyebrows went up.

"And do you know where the prince is staying? I doubt it will being whatever corner he and she were sleeping while they feigned they were common street-entertainers."

"Her Majesty offered to let them remain the night."

Marjorie nodded. When the dance ended, she took another partner and danced every dance, even once with the prince, before the clock struck midnight, when she went to bid Queen Shulamith farewell.

Queen Shulamith smiled upon her, and told her that a candleman awaited her at the door. "To get you safely home."

Marjorie thanked her and, her heart hammering, evaded both Maud and Henrietta on the way out. The candleman by the door muttered a little under his breath, and his nose was ruddy, but the candles on his hat were all brightly lit, and he led the way off steadily. Marjorie swallowed again and wondered how Queen Shulamith had known in advance that she would not leave in Maud's carriage—but she had spoken of leaving early, and rumors always spread at balls.

The lights of Queen Shulamith's ball receded behind them, and the moon shone down on them and reflected off the river when they reached it. Moths descended in silvery streams, but the enchantment on the candlelight kept even them a ways off.

The candleman began to carol an improbable ballad about a madman whom the moon had fallen in love with, and shortly thereafter, showed her to the door. The maid at the door looked startled. Then, she had to wonder at the hair, with all the fuss about the dye.

After a minute, the maid croaked, "Lady Maud?"

Marjorie blinked. Oh, yes, she had come alone and without the carriage, too.

"Is well and enjoying the ball. I returned alone rather disturb her." Marjorie glanced at the dark and silent rooms. Only a candle by the door gave any light. "The other servants ran off to a servants' ball, and left you here to let them in again?"

The maid flushed. She knew, thought Marjorie, who would be blamed.

"I won't tell Lady Maud," Marjorie said, lit her candle off the maid's, and headed up the stairs. The yellow gown came off easily, as if true cloth. She wondered how long the gown would last. . . a lavish gift, if it lasted like cloth.

The moonlight cast its light on the floor in lopsided squares, with a few moths having found their way to the glass. She snuffed the candle and went to the window before she went to bed. From it, she could still see the lights at Queen Shulamith's ball, all golden. Moths launched themselves from the now dark window. Some wavered through the air as far as the ball itself, where the dancing went on and on.

Before the sky was even gray, the first workers trudged out on the street and passed by it, and bore the news the rest of their way, that the dancers at Queen Shulamith's ball would be going to bed at dawn—

"If that," said one pastry vendor, as she handed out lukewarm meat pastries to carpenters and seamstresses plodding off to work.

"All the more work for the shoemakers," said one gray-haired seamstress, dourly, and carried the news onward. She found the servants leaving their ball, and assured them that even now they could dance the hours away without their masters' catching their mischief.

"They'll expect work to be done," said Lady Maud's cook, and with the rest, they headed back to their houses as the sky turned charcoal gray, and then paler shades. It was when they closed the door that Marjorie awoke. She looked out the window and saw it was still dove gray, with tinges of pink and yellow, and then she remembered that she had left the ball early because she needed to rise early. And why. She might have to call on the prince's favor.

Up and dressed in a respectable gray gown, she descended the stairs in search of breakfast, and servants scrambled as if caught by a sorceress. Marjorie's eyebrows went up, but she merely silently took her breakfast. And told the maid that they had to go for a walk.

The maid was silently behind her until she reached the pale house she intended. She breathed out sharply. "You can't—"

Marjorie was through the gate, passing among the statues, and up the stairs before the maid could bring herself to object. She rapped with the knocker and waited. The maid still stood by the gate. Perhaps she did not fear dismissal so much now, when Marjorie already knew how the servants had gone runagate while Queen Shulamith's ball had gone on.

The door creaked open. Michel looked up at her. Philippe half hid behind him. They still wore mourning, and still looked pale against it, but even now, she thought they had more roses in their cheeks.

"I give you good morning," she said. "I have come to see your great-great-grandfather."

"He's not here," blurted out Philippe.

"Not anywhere," said Michel, his fingers tightening on the doorknob. "We've looked. And no servants, either."

Marjorie looked between them. "That will make my case all the easier, but I will have to look myself." She stepped inside and glanced back at the gate. The maid shuddered and wrapped her shawl more closely about herself. Marjorie's eyes rolled, but she set out with the boys, upstairs and down, looking in scores of room, mostly empty, scaring up occasional cobwebs and dust, but no sign of any other human habitation, until finally they came out the backdoor, into the garden

Philippe squealed. "Look at the fishes!"

The boys scrambled over. At a more sedate pace—she had not only danced many dances, they had scrambled far, searching the house—Marjorie came over. Great enormous goldfish swam with the murky pool. Some pale with brilliantly red-gold splotches like coins, some gold as pure as a king's crown, some fiery red all over, like the sunset. The boys started to gabble something about how they had been paler, before.

"How striking," said Marjorie. "But I think it more important to deal with you." She inclined her head, and the boys looked up. "I thought to offer to take your guardianship, which is perhaps too great a burden for his years, since I am your cousin. With his having vanished like that—"

She hesitated. The boys' pale faces were utterly innocent. Perhaps later she would tell them. Now— "Come with me, then, and we will have the prince let me take it."

"Oh, can he?" said Michel.

He had better, thought Marjorie, after last night. Now, she only forced a smile and offered her hands. The boys hesitated before taking one apiece, and letting her lead them out to the street—around the house. Marvelous though Queen Shulamith's mirrors were, she did not quite trust them to unhaunt a house.

The maid blinked, but fell in behind her and the boys as they walked down the streets toward Queen Shulamith's house. Here and there, stores pulled open the doors to their wares, and Marjorie tugged the boys from the more fascinating ones. They met vendors on the way, and working folks bustling to their jobs, and even a few merchants, or housewives venturing to the stores, but only at the street itself did she see nobility as they sleepily stumbled down the stairs. She glanced sideways down the street. The coachmen looked a little more awake; she hoped they had had a chance to rest before they collided all the way down the streets.

But she could do nothing about that. She headed up the stairs as others headed down, and garnered many stares. Her gray gown stuck out among all the finery, however much the dancing had left that bedraggled, and eyebrows went up as those departing picked out the boys in their black, and yet—she set her jaw—she headed for the great doors as if there were no others.

The prince emerged, with Luc and Silvio behind him, and Gemma on his arm. She angled over.

He stopped at the sight of her. She freed her hands to curtsy, and the boys gawked for a moment and then bowed.

"I came to petition, Your Highness. These boys my cousins are the wards of their great-great-grandfather. Whose age, I dare say, made him unfit for the role, even if his family feeling made him take it on. You saw how they arrived last night—" Her words choked off, remembering the ghostly figures. She swallowed. The prince still studied her in silence. "I went to offer myself as a more hale guardian. And I found that his house had neither him, nor any of his servants—only the boys. So I brought them to petition you for their guardianship. And to take charge of the house, as part of their inheritance, if he can not be found."

No one asked why she thought the boys had inherited. They had guessed what the figures meant.

The prince smiled—and then yawned. He spoke with care. "I am glad that you have not asked for something requiring deep thought. Certainly, who could be more fit?"

Marjorie let her breath out. She still had to deal with Maud, but with the guardianship in hand, she had an argument that her aunt could not ignore.

The prince went on without pause. "And—" He glanced sideways. "I must return to my kingdom. It is not fitting that Lady Gemma should travel without a companion of noble birth."

"How true," said Marjorie. And with her hair blond again, Maud would probably be glad to see the back of her.

"There is much to be done," said the prince, meditatively. "I must start here—find a place to stay—"

"You can lease the house," said Michel, chirpily. They all looked at him. "It's all *different* now, not haunted."

"And you will charge the rent?"

Michel looked at his shoes.

Gemma cleared her throat. "We have gold enough. I saved the coins so that everyone would take us for street entertainers indeed. It would pay several months lease on even a fine home."

The prince's eyebrows went up. "You seemed to have arranged everything well."

Queen Shulamith appeared in the doorway. "Good morning," she said. "Come within, and all may be justly discussed."

Two little schoolgirls, on the way to Queen Hesione's school, watched them go in.

"They're going to add that to our lessons," said one gloomily. "The prince who was a bear and how the queen had protected him."

"We don't get to go to the ball," said the other, "but we have to *study* it."

They hurried on. From a high up window, a handful of gossips looked down from their narrow window.

"Really, this will encourage them like nothing else," said Alixandre. "Turning back into a prince and claiming the throne?"

"And," said Ida, "turning that lass into a fine lady."

Blanca lifted her cup. "Perhaps a few ladies should try fortune-telling, or dancing with bears, if they wish to mend their fortunes."

Alixandre shrugged. "So the tales have always told." She drank her tea.

Oath Keeper

Along the way, trees grew wherever men had not hewn pastures and fields from them. Sometimes so thickly that their branches left the riders in shadows near as dark as night, and here they had ridden for more than a day in such gloom.

Abruptly, the trees stopped. Scrub grew to every hand. Some bushes stood high enough to block the sight of a standing man, but most rose no higher than his knee. Hills to the north were blue but clearly visible, and Eadwin could see this wasteland held neither houses nor fields nor pasture. And few birds, which neither twittered among the branches, nor soared against the sky.

As they rode on, fewer bushes grew, and the ground had only bare rock, or low weeds. Nothing flowered.

Barren though it was, the land had many streams, making them ford the water, or running beside the way. No fish darted in them, and the plants grew no more thickly on their banks than anywhere else.

At least, Eadwin told himself, they could easily keep watch against wolves, or woodwoses. Though after a time he noted they had not seen so much as a hare.

Before full noon, a crossroads lay before them. One way turned south, and the other toward the north.

"South," said Baldwulf.

Groans came from various men in the company. Eadwin glanced at Aelfric, who shrugged. Eadwin supposed the south road could be shorter but harder. He looked back at Baldwulf, who pointed north. Eadwin scowled. A gap stood among the hills, as low as what they rode through. Or, the southerly road could be safer and longer. Men still looked sullen, but they nodded—and looked at Eadwin.

He looked at his hands for moments, and rode on with the rest. Time wound on, and still men eyed him.

The south road grew more green. They rode between great thickets of brush, though still flowerless. Baldwulf, riding forward in the company, came alongside them.

"What is the peril from the north?" said Eadwin.

Baldwulf threw his head back and laughed. It resounded. "Peril? What peril?" He shook his head and wiped his eyes. "Hear of the craft of Darkwood's thanes. Once a knight served the thane, named Eadwin. Leofwine, the knight was, and high in Eadwin's counsels. He went with other knights to hold that gap in the hills against woodwoses, as Eadwin gathered men to give them strength."

Eadwin nodded slowly and watched him with narrowed eyes.

"The woodwoses struck, and the battle was bitter. Leofwine was struck down, and lived only long enough to tell his men to bury him there, to keep the pass until Eadwin came."

Eadwin's nod came more slowly.

"The next night, the woodwoses came again, they had not slain them all the night before, and Leofwine rose up from his grave. Lit with ghost-light. Drove the woodwoses back. So—Eadwin heard of this guard, and came not as he said he would, and for generations, Leofwine has held that pass alone." He smirked. "Trapped by his own folly."

"I see," said Aelfric.

"Just three weeks ago he fought against them, and all the sky was lit with ghost-light." Baldwulf glanced over. "Saw it once when I was a child, it was like the rising moon."

Eadwin was glad the man had looked away. When Leofwine had pledged to Eadwin, being a thane, Eadwin had pledged him succor in need.

Baldwulf looked back to them. Eadwin hoped he had mastered his face.

"If you pledge to serve the thane—Osgar is Eadwin's great-great-grandson—you will find your duty lighter than under many other thanes."

"I see," said Eadwin. What sort of thane would reward such loyalty like that? he thought, and it answered itself: one whose knights found loyalty mirth and folly. "Would he want an Eadwin in his service?"

He could, he supposed, ask how long it took to find the wose woods and fell all the trees, which would end the attacks forever, but he knew that it never took even a year. So did Baldwulf.

"None of us go near," said Baldwulf. "Neither would you."

The horses clopped on.

"It's not like the land is good to farm on," said Baldwulf. And since there was no need to answer that, Eadwin did not.

After a time, when they asked no questions, Baldwulf rode toward the head of their company.

Aelfric said, his voice low, "I heard the thane—all of them since Eadwin's day—has always had hardships getting knights to serve him."

"And take his pledge?" said Eadwin, no louder. "I think that perchance, he will have no wish for me to serve him." He looked ahead. Trees stood within sight; they would reach them by nightfall, he thought. He spoke again, his voice still lower.

"Still, I would pledge to you that I will give and take no oath from any thane along this way until I reach the king's halls."

Aelfric's mouth twisted. "Only if I can pledge the same oath to you."

* * *

The next day, they rode onward with trees to either hand, and no sign of human dwellings. The day after, the trees towered for much of the day, but opened to pasture and farmland when the sky turned rose and orange. The thane's hall was large and well-built, with orchards behind it, and many beehives.

Baldwulf rode ahead of the company to tell the thane's men of his coming, and of the company he rode with. He stood in the doorway to the hall, with Osgar, a lean man with thinning brown hair and beard.

"These are the knights who traveled with you?"

Eadwin and Aelfric came forward. Youths still, and Eadwin knew that Aelfric with his golden hair and he himself with his straw-colored hair both looked younger than their age.

A young girl came out of the hall, fair-haired, pale, bearing a cup of mead. Her voice was thin as she offered it in the name of Osgar her father and Begilda her mother, to make them welcome. A woman, her fair-hair threaded with white, watched like a hawk from behind her, and sent the girl back to her bower as soon as they had drunk, before she turned to them and asked of their names and households.

"I am Aelfric son of Beorn," said Aelfric, "and my companion is Eadwin son of Ceolfrith. We both come from the Seaward Lands, where our fathers' lands bordered one another, but we travel together because I am a fourth son, and he a third, and our elder brothers have sons of their own."

"I have heard of such lands," said Osgar. "I have heard of boats that the nicor would attack."

Eadwin laughed, low in his throat. "And a knight must follow them into the water to slay them. Many other knights did as well as we two, to rid the sea of them."

"Far better to hunt the boar and deer in the forest," said Aelfric. "We did many a time."

"I can offer you fair hunting in this land," said Osgar, lightly. "I go to hunt within a week, and welcome you are to stay the time."

Eadwin opened his mouth, and shut it again. To go hunting was not a pledge. Still—"I have pledged to ride on until I reach the king's hall."

"As have I," said Aelfric.

A booming laugh sounded behind Osgar. Another knight came from the hall, his face ruddy as a drunkard.

"What southern soppiness is this? What decadent, milksop fool takes an oath about such thing?" He leaned forward, blinking, to peer at them. "Or bothers to treat it as an oath?" He hiccuped. "There's men who call themselves knights down south who swore never to wield another sword until they recovered a lost one—cowards, all of them—that's why they don't know a knight in battle, but dub them—" He looked baffled for a moment, as if he forgot who stood before him.

"Come in," said Begilda. "Let us eat."

* * *

Three days later, the king's hall stood at the height of the hill, and seven roads led through the lands toward it. They had ridden in settled lands all that day.

Aelfric and Eadwin rode toward it, past pastures filled with cattle for the feast, past the clanging smithy, past a stream lined with laundresses at work.

At the door, the king's daughter Goldborough, her hair falling in two golden plaits, came forward, bearing the cup of mead, more kindly and more at ease than Osgar's daughter. And Theodoric King, still great as bear though his golden hair was touched with silver, made them welcome and asked of the battle with the nicors, saying only rumors had reached them, and listened gravely to the tale.

"Two such knights to serve a thane would do much to aid the land's peace."

For all he had left his father's house to search for a thane to serve, Eadwin's heart beat fast at the thought of it.

"Many thanes serve as the march wardens of the lands. You have come by the hall of Osgar."

Aelfric's face contorted, and smoothed out. "When I spoke with the knights there, they assured me that there was less fighting that for many other thanes. Less honor to be won in serving such a knight." He turned to Eadwin, his face confident.

"I will go to Osgar," said Eadwin.

Aelfric blinked.

"I wish to rest from my journey," he said. "But I will leave on the morrow."

* * *

Rain whispered on the needles of the firs and drummed on the road. Puddles and mud spread all before him. Flat gray clouds spread over every gap in the branches. The storm neither thundered nor blew with strong winds, but it rained without end. His horse's head hung, and most of the ride, his did as well.

Three days out, three days back, thought Eadwin. Heaven's King grant that he could make time as good on this way.

But no better.

The road went down the hillside, with rivulets flowing by the horse's hooves. The stream that had flowed easily before, and formed wide pools, now roared with waters, and flowed with white foam.

The bridge slowly came into view. Great tangles of wood stood before him, and he pulled up his horse. For a moment, his heart seemed dead in his chest, and he thought the bridge gone. Then it hammered. A great mass of deadwood, borne downstream, had struck the bridge. The logs of it were cracked on that side. But—

He rode onward, as slowly as he could. The horse snorted and rolled its eyes. At the bridge, for a moment he thought of urging it onward. Then he snorted, dismounted, and went to lead it.

Branches reached out toward them, making the sound part of the bridge like walking through bramble. His heart hammered every moment, but finally, he reached the other side and led the horse off. His heart lightened.

The rain thickened. It hammered on the bridge, and the wood groaned. It did not lessen his cheer as he mounted again and rode off.

* * *

His daughter bore out the cup again, and Begilda looked anxious.

"Osgar my husband has gone hunting," she said in haste.

Eadwin nodded. "Even as he said. If the rains had not hindered my way, I might have reached here in time. Perhaps you could tell me which way he and his company rode?"

She told him. He nodded, glad that it was northerly, and rode far enough in that direction to be sure that no one marked him when he turned his way.

* * *

There would be no hunting in this bare land of stone and bramble, Eadwin thought. Unless Osgar came hunting him. He had dared carry only a little food, lest the king guess his intent, and remember what care he had taken with his words.

The sunlight shone down on the waste as he rode. And rode. He still rode when the sky turned scarlet and orange in the west, and he knew he would not reach the gap by sunset. He glanced east, where the moon rose, enormous and glowing yellow against the darkening blue. He would cease when he feared for his horse's footing.

But it had been four weeks, more or less, since the woodwoses had attacked. If Baldwulf had told the truth. Nearly the full turn of the moon. The woodwoses could attack again, and soon. Even if they could also forbear for a season or two.

His mouth twisted. Or find another path around the hills and attack Osgar in his hall.

He rode on, more slowly. The evening stars gleamed, the sunset faded, the moon rose. The brambles, low though they were, cast many shadows, and when he rode onto a stretch of bare rock, Eadwin decided to sleep there. The way on was too dark. He dismounted.

Light flared ahead, more swiftly than a bonfire leaping up. His head turned away, and his arm flew up to shield his eyes, and he stood there blinking before it came to him that the light had shone blue, and bestial shrieks and howls were resounding.

Slowly, he lowered his arm. His eyes could endure the light, which did glow as blue as as the summer sky, flaring up from the earth. He swallowed. It was not that far ahead.

His horse was stiff and still. For a moment, without thinking, he went to mount again, but the horse shuddered. After a moment, he bound the reins to the nearest bramble, and ran. Not for a moment did the sound of howls cease. And other sounds of battle, though not the clash of metal.

Between one briar and the next, the path dipped into a hollow, and all within was lit by blue light. Scores of woodwoses already lay on the ground, their ragged fur matted with darkness that could not look red in this light, but scores more attacked a lone figure, who cast no shadow. His face was set in lines of exhaustion and despair as his sword cut down woodwose after woodwose.

Eadwin drew his sword and ran.

The nearest woodwose turned its bestial face from Leofwine, and bared its fangs to snarl at Eadwin, but it had not turned to guard against him. It fell easily. Howls of rage rose from the nearest, and in a moment, he found himself attacked. Not one had the patience to circle about him, and only that saved him as their claws tore toward him. Every one he struck hard enough to fell was trampled by another, eager to reach him.

He eased his way back. His first blows had taken down woodwoses because they had not defended themselves. They would get around him without thinking as they snarled and snapped and clawed. . . .

His foot caught on a stone, and he sprawled against the earth. His sword jolted from his hands, and skittered downhill. A woodwose seized its hilt and snapped it in two.

For a moment, he could not breathe. He had killed himself. Unarmed, against woodwoses with inhuman strength—the only mercy was that he had made no pledge to stay—

"Here!"

Something flashed through the air, landed beside his hand, and came clear as a sword. He snatched it up and struck.

The woodwose before him lost its hand as the blade sliced easily through the arm, as though it were no more than cheese. The woodwose shrieked to the moon. Others snarled, and Eadwin leapt to the attack. The moon had not risen much farther before he stood, alone, panting, where every woodwose had fallen, no sign of the other knight was to be seen, and the blue light was fading away.

He staggered across the hollow toward where the other knight had stood. Bones lay there, unburied, and the rusty remains of a sword. A familiar sword.

Eadwin felt cold. He looked down at the blade. It seemed like a true sword, and not the ghost of one.

If it lasted until morning—

He shook his head. For now he would build a cairn from the loose stone; he could not dig a grave. And after, there would be more for him to do.

* * *

The king's hall was filled with grim-faced thanes and knights, and others who came to see his judgment on his wayward knight. Baldwulf stood, indignant, by the king's right hand, ready to press his thane's claim.

Theodoric's voice boomed from the roof. "Did you not pledge to me that you would pledge to Osgar?"

"No," said Eadwin. He stood rigidly straight. "I told you I would go to Osgar. And so I did. I pledged no more to you, I pledged nothing to him."

Silence followed. Theodoric studied him with narrowed eyes. At least he had not falsely claimed that Eadwin had made that pledge. But he had not made his judgment.

Said Eadwin, "He owed me nothing as well. Not succor in need."

For a moment, he stood there, his heart hammering.

Then Theodoric laughed, and all about, thanes and knights and the king's wife and sons and daughters, and all the other men and women, roared with laughter.

"Ho, Baldwulf," said Theodoric. "Tell your thane not to expect service from men not pledged to serve him."

"And that is the end of that?" said Baldwulf. "To leave that land open and defenseless? What of what you pledged to Osgar, o king?"

"Succor in need!" said Theodoric. "I will give him it. A man with a ghostly sword will guard him still." He turned his head. "Eadwin, I grant to you all the wasteland about the pass where the ghost stood guard. To hold and to defend from all fell creatures, so that they fall on no other land."

Eadwin bowed, quickly, to hide his face. He strode forward to go to his knees and pledge to hold the lands, and be Theodoric's man.

As they went to the feast, after, Aelfric came to him, and said, "A thane needs knights."

"So he does," said Eadwin merrily, and only then realized that three other men had followed Aelfric.

"These are the great-grandsons of Leofwine," said Aelfric. "They, too, look for a thane, as I do."

All four men looked grim-faced.

"You will find it better even than you think," said Eadwin.

He found himself less merry as they pledged to him, and he swore to be their liege, to provide and protect, to succor in need.

Then he told them to be ready within a day.

* * *

The younger sons of freeholders, also, needed lands, and he led a company of a score of them as they rode out to the waste.

Or where the waste had been. Already brambles showed more greenery, and some bore roses white or pink, and some stretches, where there had been only earth before, had grown grass.

Eadwin, who had felt smug in the forest, let out his breath slowly. It had not been a week since he had freed Leofwine. Even the first day, even at dawn, the colors in the sky had found the first blossoms on the waste, but he had not expected this flourishing.

Birds. Birds flitted and flew everywhere.

Finally, at noon—"Why?" said Aelfric. "You can not have unleashed some spellcraft on the land. The woodwose could not have blighted it."

Eadwin said, slowly, "It was the land that a dead man guarded. How could it flourish?" And now it flourished as if it wished to regrow in a year what it had lost in a century.

One freeman said, "We will have to set border stones, to mark the boundaries of your land."

"So we shall," said Eadwin. "But first we need to make haste. There is still the wose wood ahead. We must fell it."

"You have to find it first," said the oldest of the brothers, also Leofwine.

"So we will," said Eadwin, lightly, but the hollow was ahead. He rode in. Grass had grown thickly, and a wildflower had grown, creeping, over Leofwine's grave, and flowered with dainty red blooms. He lowered his head a moment, but then he rode on. The hollow led out to a larger valley, also blighted by the ghostly guard, except for one stand of trees in it.

Leofwine snorted. "Time for axes?"

"O yes," said Eadwin. "And—" He pointed at the other end of the valley, where the hills narrowed about it. "That is where we build the fortress to protect this all. My lands."

"It will need it," said Aelfric, smiling. "Fell creatures will endanger so fair a land."

Also by Mary Catelli

Curses And Wonders
Dragon Slayer
Eyes of the Sorceress
Fever and Snow
Mermaids' Song
Sword and Shadow
The Book of Bone
Witch-Prince Ways
Dragonfire and Time
Enchantments And Dragons
Jewel of the Tiger
Over the Sea, To Me
The Dragon's Cottage
The Maze, the Manor, and the Unicorn
The White Menagerie
A Diabolical Bargain
Madeleine and the Mists
Magic And Secrets
The Lion and the Library
The Princess Goes Into The Forest
The Wolf and the Ward
The Witch-Child and the Scarlet Fleet
Treachery And Spells
Winter's Curse
Crow Curse

Free Passage
Isabelle and the Siren
Journeys And Wizardry
Lifestone
Magic of the Lost God
Never Comment On A Likeness
One Name
The Drunken Mermaids
The Turtle in the Sea of Sand
Were I You
Where There Is Smoke
Through A Mirror, Darkly
The Princess Seeks Her Fortune
Sorcery and Kings

About the Author

Mary Catelli is an avid reader of fantasy, science fiction, history, fairy tales, philosophy, folklore and a lot of other things. (Including the backs of cereal boxes.) Which, in due course, overflowed into writing fantasy (and some science fiction).

www.ingramcontent.com/pod-product-compliance
Lightning Source LLC
Chambersburg PA
CBHW060824120626
46557CB00001B/365